RASPBERRY ONE

RASPBERRY ONE
CHARLES FERRY

HOUGHTON MIFFLIN COMPANY
BOSTON

The U.S.S. *Shiloh,* Wickford College, and the Naval
hospital described in Part Three of this book, though
representative of the era, are fictional creations.

Library of Congress Cataloging in Publication Data

Ferry, Charles, 1927–
   Raspberry One.

   Summary: Nick and Hildy, two young aircrewmen flying
bombing support against Japan's kamikaze offensive in
the Pacific, are devastated but ultimately strengthened
by their war experience.
   1. World War, 1939–1945 — Pacific Ocean — Juvenile
fiction. [1. World War, 1939–1945 — Pacific Ocean —
Fiction. 2. World War, 1939–1945 — Aerial operations.
3. Friendship — Fiction] I. Title.
PZ7.F42Ras 1983   [Fic]   82-25476
ISBN 0-395-34069-1

Copyright © 1983 by Charles Ferry

Printed in the United States of America

VB 10 9 8 7 6 5 4

TO SISTER AGATHA

TABLE OF CONTENTS

I remember my youth and the feeling that will never come back . . . the feeling that I could last forever, outlast the sea, the earth, and all men; the deceitful feeling that lures us on to joys, to perils, to love, to vain effort — to death . . .

— Joseph Conrad
Youth

PART ONE: THE GOOD TIMES

1. FRANNY

WHEN IT WAS OVER, WHAT THEY REMEM-
bered most about that bittersweet Rhode Island autumn
was the parties. Parties at the Knickerbocker, at the little
downstairs bar at the Biltmore, at the casino on Narragansett Bay where they danced to an orchestra with five
saxophones. They did crazy things. Nick, on a dare, once
carried Franny across the lobby of the Parker House on
his shoulders. That was the day they all went up to Boston for the Harvard-Bates game. They had beer at a student hangout and scrod at a Back Bay restaurant, and on
the trip back to Providence, Diane and Hildy jitter-
bugged in the club car of the train — Hildy, in dress
blues, cheerful, uncomplicated, looking as though he'd
just stepped out of a Navy recruiting poster; and Diane,
impulsive, moody, excitingly pretty, never wanting the
fun to end.

And if there was a desperate quality to their merry-
making, it was 1944, and there was a sense of time running
out — Nick and Hildy, crewmen on a Navy torpedo
bomber, soon to ship out to the Pacific, where the Japanese had launched a kamikaze offensive; Franny and
Diane, sophomores at Wickford, the girls they would
leave behind.

It had begun with a wartime strand of circumstance,
an invitation posted on the bulletin board of the squadron ready room.

The Students and Faculty of
WICKFORD COLLEGE
Cordially Invite the
PILOTS AND AIRCREWMEN
of
TORPEDO SQUADRON 43
to a
RECEPTION AND TEA
Sunday, September 24, 1944
Three O'Clock, in the Refectory
The favor of a reply is requested.

"Actually, Diane and I were going to stay in our room and study," Franny said afterward. "But we decided it would be unpatriotic."

"What she means," Diane explained, "is that we were afraid you'd turn out to be a bunch of drips."

Ironically, Nick and Hildy had also made other plans, but Mr. Scott — Lieutenant Commander Scott — had been firm.

"Those girls have probably worked hard on this," he said. "It would be an insult to snub them."

And so, in the end, VT-43 attended in full force, sixteen pilots and thirty-two aircrewmen, shoes shined and uniforms pressed, feeling a bit ill at ease in the oak-paneled refectory, with the rustle of skirts and the murmur of girlish voices all around them.

Nick and Hildy and Mr. Scott had scarcely entered the room when two girls came up to them.

"Hello," said one of them nervously. 'I'm Fr-franny Kaplan, and this is Diane Webb. We've got some delicious punch, if you'd care for a cup."

("I felt so embarrassed," Franny said later. "Diane put me up to it. She'd caught a glimpse of Hildy and wanted to head the other girls off at the pass.")

Diane was a revelation, a breathtakingly pretty girl, with long blond hair and an intimate quality in her voice that hinted of gaiety and romance. But what was most striking was her resemblance to Hildy, the same blue eyes, blond hair, fair skin. Franny was fascinated.

"I don't believe it," she said as Diane led Hildy to the punch bowl. "They're a matched pair."

"Diane isn't from Minnesota, by any chance?" Mr. Scott inquired.

"No. New Britain, Connecticut," Franny replied. "But they could pass for twins, couldn't they?"

Nick, however, was paying little attention to Diane. He had been immediately drawn to Franny — her dark eyes, her warm manner, her habit of tilting her head slightly as she listened to you. He liked the way she accepted her roommate's striking looks, without envy or resentment. She was wearing a green cardigan over a white round-collared blouse, with a gray flannel skirt, scuffed loafers — and knee socks.

"Visitors always ask about them," she said when Mr. Scott remarked that nearly all the girls seemed to be wearing them. "They're a school trademark — you know, like blazers at Smith." She smiled. "You can always tell a Wickford girl by her knee socks."

And then Diane was back from the punch bowl, Hildy in tow, with a barrage of questions, which Mr. Scott handled as best he could. Nick was from Philadelphia, he told her; Rittenhouse Square. His father was a lawyer, and he'd been accepted at Princeton before being called up by the Navy. Hildy was from Red Wing, a small town in Minnesota. He'd enlisted right out of high school, and had never been east before. Mr. Scott himself was from New York City, Brooklyn Heights, from a family in which Annapolis was a tradition. Their squadron, VT-43 ("*V* for heavier than air," he said, carefully explaining the designations. "*T* for torpedo."), was a part of Carrier Air Group 43 (CAG), which also included a bombing squadron (VB) and a fighter squadron (VF), for a total of ninety aircraft. Their plane was a single-engine, three-man TBF (*T* for torpedo, *B* for bomber, *F* for Grumman, the manufacturer). Hildy was the turret gunner; Nick was the radioman and tail gunner and also operated the radar.

"There's a shortwave set in the dorm that picks up planes from the air station," Diane said. "Maybe we'll be able to hear you on the radio."

"Listen for 'Raspberry One,' " Hildy said.

"What's that?" Franny asked.

"Our plane," Hildy said. " 'Raspberry' because that's the squadron's code name, and 'One' because Mr. Scott is the commanding officer."

"How wonderful!" Diane exclaimed. She cupped her hands over her mouth and mimicked a radio transmission. "Hello, tower. Hello, tower. This is Raspberry One. Send up some whipped cream."

That was Diane.

"Does your plane have an insignia?" she asked Mr. Scott.

"No," he replied. "We've never been able to think of one."

"Good," she said. "I'll design one for you."

That too was Diane — quickly shifting moods, from clown to serious artist in a wink. Her father, they learned, operated the biggest real estate company in New Britain, and every summer the family packed her off to a fine arts camp in the Poconos. Franny had grown up in an apartment on the East Side of Manhattan, Seventy-first Street. Her mother had died five years ago; her two older brothers were in the Army, one on General Marshall's staff; and her father was a physician, a rather successful one, Nick gathered, since Franny said he consulted at hospitals in other parts of the country.

"Are you an art major, too?" he asked her.

"No," she said. "Literature. I'd like to work in publishing. Not as a writer; I've got no talent for that. But I think I'd make a good editor."

There was a brief welcoming speech by the dean, who asked everyone in the squadron to sign a special guest register, which would be filed in the library.

"This is a very special occasion for Wickford College," the dean said, "and we want to record it for posterity."

When refreshments were served, Franny and Diane took plates for Nick and Hildy to a special table, next to a window that looked out on the main quad. As the four of them ate, the faculty string ensemble played a Schubert quartet, and then a student combo entertained with Glenn Miller selections.

"Hey, that reminds me — " Hildy said, consuming his sixth sandwich. "There's a band at the Starlite Casino with a sax section almost as good as Glenn Miller's. Maybe we could all go dancing some Saturday."

"After sundown?" Diane asked.

Hildy expected a joke. "Okay, I'll bite," he said. "Why after sundown?"

"Saturday is Franny's Sabbath," Diane said.

"I don't understand." He was puzzled. "Sunday is the Sabbath, isn't it?"

"Franny is Jewish, Hildy," Nick said.

With anyone else, it might have been a disaster, but Hildy was without guile.

"No kidding, Franny?" he said with genuine interest. "Hey, how about that." And then he was telling her about the Jewish girl he'd once had a crush on back in Red Wing, and she was telling him about Rosh Hashanah and Yom Kippur and the observance of the Jewish Sabbath.

"Well," he said finally. "If Saturdays aren't convenient, what about a Friday?"

Franny tilted her head and smiled. "Before sundown?" she said.

They all laughed.

Hildy's invitation was left hanging, and Nick concluded that they'd been turned down. But when a Navy bus arrived to take the squadron back to Quonset Point, he had a few minutes alone with Franny, walking across the campus in the autumn dusk.

"About the casino — " she said, lowering her eyes. "Next Saturday would be fine. I mean, if you and Hildy were serious."

"Of course we were serious."

"Good." She smiled. "And don't worry about sundown. It's difficult to be observant about religion at school."

"I know," Nick said. "It seems I'm always missing Mass in the Navy."

"Are you a serious Catholic?" she asked.

"Yes, I suppose I am. I went to Saint Crispin's. I was an altar boy and led the Rosary."

"That's nice," she said. "It's important to have strong ties."

They had reached the bus.

"Well," she said, and extended her hand shyly, "until next Saturday?"

"I'll be looking forward to it." Nick held her hand a moment longer than was necessary. "And thank you. We had a wonderful time."

Franny and Diane waved as the bus pulled away.

"They're really nice girls, aren't they, Nick?" Hildy said.

"Yes," Nick agreed. "They're special."

"I can't get over those knee socks. The girls back home never wear them."

"Haven't you heard?" Nick said, smiling. "You can always tell a Wickford girl by her knee socks."

He felt very good. They had met two great girls. There would be warmth and laughter before they sailed.

2. An Unavoidable Reality

THEY BECAME A FOURSOME, GOING EVERY-where together, doing special things, discovering special places.

"We drink too much and smoke too much," Franny remarked the night they crashed a party at the Knicker-bocker. "We'll never survive the war."

Which wasn't entirely accurate. Hildy, in his wholesome Midwestern way, didn't smoke — at least not at first — and drank only an occasional beer, sometimes a glass of wine.

"Who needs liquor?" he would say. "I get high just watching the rest of you."

And thus he was relied on to make sure he and Nick got the girls back to the dorm on time, taking charge of the trip to Wickford as he took charge of all their excursions — collecting their coats, taking care of the check, hustling them to the door.

"But I haven't finished my drink," Diane would squeal.

"One sip," he would say. "You've got five seconds."

And then a mad dash through the streets of downtown Providence to catch the commuter train to Wickford, which was fifteen miles down Narragansett Bay, within view of the Naval Air Station at Quonset Point, where Nick and Hildy were stationed. The rickety coaches were so poorly heated you could see your breath, which gave them an excuse to snuggle intimately in the dim light, paired off in separate seats but exchanging amusing remarks across the aisle, whispered nonsense coming from Diane, more serious conversation from Franny, the practical one. Had they written to their mothers? Would their letters be censored in the Pacific? Had there been any word about the *Shiloh*, the aircraft carrier to which their squadron had been assigned? The *Shiloh*, which had taken two torpedoes in the Marianas and was undergoing repairs at Norfolk, was a constant presence to them, clouding every party, every kiss.

"You're a worrywart," Nick told Franny the night they decided their future.

"Perhaps," she admitted. "But it's a nice kind of worry. Do you mind?"

"No. It's been growing on me. Everything about you has been growing on me."

"I know," she said without looking at him. "It's been that way with me."

"Enough to consider a mixed marriage?"

She fidgeted with the fingers of her woolen gloves. "Yes," she said quietly.

Nick turned in his seat to face her. "Franny," he said, "I don't think you realize what I just asked you."

"Of course I do, silly." She smiled and gave him a quick kiss. "I thought you'd never get around to it."

"Well, I'll be — " Nick said, and they both laughed.

"I'm glad it happened this way," she said. "No fuss, no fanfare. Your going off to war is all I can handle at the moment."

"There'll be problems," Nick said. "What about your family?"

"I'm not sure. My father will be upset, of course. Any Jewish father would be, when his daughter announces that she's going to marry a Roman Catholic. But he's a very kind man, and if he's sure it's what I want, he might accept it."

"And your brothers?"

"That's another matter. They sometimes feel very strongly about religion."

"I'll have to get you a ring."

"No, not yet, Nickie. Let's just put it all aside and make the most of the time you've got left." She unbuttoned his pea coat and slipped her arm around his waist. "Besides, I don't need a ring. You'll find that I make very strong commitments."

Wickford was one of a string of villages that dotted the western shore of the bay, midway between Providence and Point Judith, where the bay emptied into the Atlantic. A taxi service operated from the depot, but they preferred to walk the half mile to the campus, along a country road lined by trees with gnarled trunks. Diane and Hildy, full of energy, would run on ahead, kicking up the fallen leaves, which, in late October, lay ankle-deep on the road. It was a very old school. A weathered statue of Elisha Wickford, who had purchased the site from the Narragansett Indians in the seventeenth century, stood in the center of the main quadrangle. Ivy grew on the walls of the library, and behind the Humanities Building, a woodland path led to a sheltered promontory — "the Point" — that overlooked the bay. It was there that they ended their evenings, in hurried embraces under the stars, secluded from the giggles and stares of the other Wickford girls, to whom Diane and Franny had become an item of gossip.

"I feel cheated," Diane joked one night. "I'm getting a reputation without the fun."

"I'd be glad to correct that situation for you," Hildy said, baring his teeth like a vampire and pulling her toward the trees. "Come into my lair, *Liebchen* — "

"Hildy, don't you dare!" Diane squealed — and they were off running again, through the trees and across the quad, their laugher floating on the cool night air.

Nick and Franny watched with smiles.

"They're a pair, aren't they?" Franny said, shaking her head. "I'm surprised they haven't eloped by now."

"Then it's really serious with Diane?" Nick said.

"Very. Diane's trouble is, she's too pretty for her own good. Boys either want to sleep with her or parade her around like an ornament. Hildy's the first one who's accepted her for herself."

"That's Hildy. His charm is that he has no charm."

"Yes, that's true," Franny said. "It's funny. He was the reason our foursome got started, really — the sophisticated Easterners showing off to the small-town boy from Minnesota, dragging him to plays and concerts and night-clubs. And it ended up with all of us leaning on him. You look to him for leadership. Diane can't get through the day unless she sees him or talks to him on the phone. And I lean on him to look after you when the two of you are on those bombing and strafing exercises out over the ocean."

"That's very perceptive."

"No, it isn't perceptive at all. I don't believe in ana-lyzing relationships." She took his hand and squeezed it. "I'd much rather just live them."

As the weeks went by, the Point increasingly became a refuge for them, a place to escape the uncertainties of war and to mark the changing season. The brilliance of October gave way to the cold rains and gray skies of No-vember. There was a light snowfall on the first day of December, and the *Providence Journal* warned of a hard winter.

"That's one thing about the South Pacific," Hildy said, always seeing a bright side to things. "No snow."

Yet even at the Point, the war was always at hand. On cloudy nights, the sky glowed from the lights of the vast Naval complex that extended the length of the bay — the fleet base at Newport, the air station, the sprawling supply depot at Davisville. Destroyers moved up and down the bay at regular intervals, leaving on or return-ing from sub patrol; and on land, Coast Guard sentries with rifles and attack dogs patrolled the shoreline. One night, under a bright moon, Franny led Nick down to the place in the jagged rocks where the body of a German officer had washed up early in the war, when Nazi wolf packs were roaming freely in coastal waters.

"His submarine had been sunk off Point Judith,"

she said. "He was still wearing his hat, an overseas cap with a swastika emblem. The dean kept it as a souvenir. It's in the trophy case in the Main Hall."

"Did any subs ever come this far up the bay?" Nick asked.

"No one knows," Franny said, "but everybody was afraid they would. Wild rumors went around — that a ticket stub to a Providence movie theater had been found in the German's pocket. That subs were surfacing every night to let the sailors go ashore and drink beer. That a dairy in Warwick was supplying them with fresh milk and eggs."

"That's hilarious," Nick said.

"I know," Franny said, "but a lot of people believed it. I wasn't here then, but the seniors brought us down here when we were freshmen and scared us to death with stories about it. It made the war seem very close, and now when I see newsreels of the war zones I feel I know what it's like — thousands of refugees clogging the roads, with nothing to eat and no place to sleep. And we complain about a shortage of nylons and cigarettes. It must be even worse in the concentration camps. My father is very worried about what's happening to the Jews."

"Do you have any relatives over there?"

"All Jews have relatives over there," Franny said. "And my father has close friends at the medical school in Heidelberg. He's afraid they've been killed, but it's hard to get information. He's on a committee. They're trying to see President Roosevelt."

"He sounds like quite a guy."

"He is. When he was in college, he used to go downtown at night to teach English to immigrants. He was just a little boy when my grandparents came over from the Ukraine, but he'd never forgotten their struggles with the language. I hope you'll get to meet him before you leave."

Hildy's birthday, December 8, fell on a Friday, a twelve o'clock night for the girls. They celebrated with dinner in Providence, at an Italian place up the street from Union Station, and then had drinks at their favorite spot — the downstairs bar at the Biltmore Hotel, an intimate, low-ceilinged room, done in rich woods, with leather chairs grouped around a fireplace and, behind the bar, a large mural of Falstaff and his companions, painted by a famous artist. Diane, the art major, could never pass the mural without gazing at it with envy.

"Such depth," she would say. "Such texture. One day I'm going to paint like that."

They ordered schooners of ale, which they drank at a copper-topped table in front of the fireplace. Hildy was all butterfingers as he opened his gifts. There was a pair of silver aircrewman's wings from Nick; a copy of *A Bell for Adano*, one of the new best sellers, from Franny ("It's hard to choose gifts for servicemen," she said, "but you ought to have plenty of reading time aboard ship"); and, from Diane, a silver ID bracelet, inscribed *To H from D, 12-8-44, with L.* As they all fussed over the bracelet, a voice behind Hildy said: "I heard you mention you'd be coming here. I thought you wouldn't mind if I dropped by — "

It was Lieutenant Commander Scott, looking every inch the career officer, Annapolis '39, a veteran of the Guadalcanal and Gilbert Islands campaigns, and a man on his way up in the Navy.

"Hey, what a swell surprise!" exclaimed Hildy, who idolized Mr. Scott. "Nick, look who's here" — and he signaled the waiter for another chair.

Even though they enjoyed a close personal relationship with their pilot, Nick and Hildy observed strict Naval etiquette. They would never have dreamed of calling him "Bob." On or off the base, he was "Mr. Scott" or "Commander Scott" or, in the air, "Skipper," and Diane and Franny addressed him with the same respect.

"It's nice to see you again, Commander Scott," Diane said. "The girls are still talking about the reception."

"Thank you, Diane," Mr. Scott said. "That was a very nice affair."

A tall, gangling man with a quiet air of authority, he towered over Nick and Hildy, each of whom was five-ten, the maximum height for torpedo bomber aircrewmen because of the cramped crew stations in the TBF Avenger, their plane.

"I don't have the kind of birthday gift you can wrap," he said, and took an official Navy envelope from the inside pocket of his blue tunic. "But this document says that Philip Hildebrandt, otherwise known as Hildy, is now an aviation ordnanceman first class, and that Nicholas Enright, Nick to his friends, is an aviation radioman second class."

Hildy let out a yell. "Did you hear that, Nick? We've been promoted!"

"But Hildy still outranks you, Nick," Diane chided him. "You'll never catch up."

"He ought to," Nick said. "He set a record at aerial gunnery school that still stands. Seventeen percent hits."

"And what did you score?" Franny asked him.

"I barely qualified," he answered. "But I'm pretty good at Morse code."

Mr. Scott started to get up.

"Well, I'd better be on my way," he said.

"No, please, Mr. Scott, not yet," Franny said, and whispered something to their waiter who disappeared

into the kitchen briefly and returned with a small birthday cake, devil's food with butter cream frosting, decorated with nineteen candles.

"A cake!" Hildy said in amazement. "How the
heck — "

"We had it all arranged," Franny said, smiling. "Now
blow out the candles."

Hildy blew them out in one puff.

"Tell us what you wished," Diane said.

"It's sort of private."

"Pretty please," she coaxed.

"Okay. I wished that a certain girl with long blond
hair would give me nineteen birthday kisses."

Diane blushed. "Here's one on account," she said,
giving him a quick kiss on the cheek. "You can collect
the rest later."

Finally, the party began to wind down. Mr. Scott was
the first to leave.

"Don't stay up too late," he said to Nick and Hildy.
"We've got an early flight in the morning. Mock torpedo
runs off Cape Cod."

"He's so nice," Franny said when Mr. Scott had gone.
"How did he manage to pick you two for his crew?"

"He didn't," Nick said. "We picked him. That's the
way it works in the Navy — the aircrewmen choose their
pilot. It's supposed to promote better teamwork."

"It was his combat experience that swayed us," Hildy
added. "We figured we'd have a better chance of staying
alive with him than with some greenhorn."

"Don't say things like that, Hildy," Diane said,
frowning. "Of course you're going to stay alive."

"Of course," Hildy said, and grinned. "And Mr.
Scott is our insurance."

It was snowing when they left the Biltmore, lightly

at first, more heavily when the commuter train arrived in Wickford — thick, wet flakes that clung to the trees and gave a fairyland quality to the village and the rolling hills surrounding it. Diane was exhilarated.

"Isn't it lovely?" she said, lifting her face to the snow. "It tickles your nose."

She grabbed Hildy, and the two of them danced up the road, in a wide, sweeping waltz that left patterns in the snow.

"See you later," she called back to Nick and Franny. "We're going to do some snow sculpture."

By the time Nick and Franny reached the Point, Hildy had made the beginnings of a fat snowman. Diane was scooping up armloads of snow on the edge of the promontory.

"I'm going to do a dolphin," she said. "Curved very gracefully, as if it's leaping from the water — "

And as she said that, she suddenly dropped the snow and pointed toward the bay.

"Oh, my God!" she said with a gasp. "Look at the size of that ship."

Through the swirling snow, they could make out the dark bulk of an enormous ship inching up the bay. It was at least three hundred yards long and towered a hundred feet or more above the water. The huge starboard funnel provided unmistakable identification. It was one of the most venerable ships in the history of the United States Navy, the largest and fastest American aircraft carrier ever built, with an unmatched combat record — the Coral Sea, Midway, Guadalcanal, Tarawa, Saipan.

"It's the *Shiloh*," Hildy said in a small voice. "I had no idea she was so big."

They watched in silence as the great ship vanished in the snow. Diane was the first to speak.

"Just when you think you've got your life all arranged . . ." she said, her voice trailing off.

"Aw, come on, Diane," Hildy said, trying to reassure her. "Nothing's really final yet. The Japs could surrender before we sail, or we could be assigned to the Atlantic Fleet and be in port twice a month."

"You don't expect me to believe that," she said tightly. "I read the papers, Hildy. The German Navy's finished. It's the Pacific where the carriers are needed, because the kamikazes are sinking so many of them. What can you do against a suicide plane, for God's sake?"

She began crying.

"Hey, there's nothing to cry about," Hildy said. "Everything's going to be okay. You'll see."

"No, Hildy, it's not. I have a feeling. Sometimes when I kiss you I think I'm kissing a future corpse."

Hildy's head jerked back as though he'd been struck, and for the first time in their long friendship, Nick thought he saw clouds of doubt in his eyes.

"I'm sorry, Hildy." Diane wiped her eyes with her mittens. "I shouldn't have said those awful things."

"It's okay," Hildy said. "What people don't realize is, most of the guys that go into combat come out of it without a scratch."

"My high school French teacher didn't," Diane said. "He was at Anzio. We went to visit him at an Army hospital in Boston. I nearly threw up when I saw his face."

She was crying again. Hildy put an arm around her, and they started down to the dorm.

"She upset you," Franny said to Nick, "didn't she?"

"A little," Nick said. "It was so out of character."

"Not really. You've got to live with Diane to know her. She feels things but never lets on."

Nick had a nervous feeling in his stomach. Diane

had alluded to possibilities that he had purposely shut from his mind. For the first time, he was afraid of the war. He felt like getting drunk.

"Shouldn't you be getting back, too?" he said to Franny.

"In a minute," she said. "After you've kissed me good night."

It was a long, lingering kiss. Normally, their passion was cautious and restrained. There were rules, standards. Franny was hardly a girl for a few hours in some walk-up hotel. Which really didn't matter; Nick was totally inexperienced in walk-up hotels. What mattered was the possibility that something might go wrong, and then where would they be? But now the rules and standards failed him, and his hands were all over her, urgently, insistently.

"We really shouldn't be doing this," she whispered.

"I know," he mumbled, fumbling with her coat.

"Oh, God, Nickie, no one's ever touched me there before."

"I'm sorry."

"No, don't be." She covered his face with feathery kisses. "I'll sleep with you whenever you want, but I hope you can wait. I'm really a very traditional girl."

Nick's whole body tingled. It was the most exciting thing that had ever happened to him. He started to say something, something tender and romantic, but just then Franny spotted the dormitory lights blinking through the trees and broke away.

"I've got to hurry or I'll get demerits." She gave him a final kiss and ran down the path. "Call me tomorrow. We'll meet in the village."

Nick slumped against a tree, his thoughts whirling in confusion. He was barely nineteen years of age that night, as were the others. But it seemed to him that their lives were out of control, that the war was cheating them of their youth and rushing them toward — who could say? He had wanted to avoid entanglements. That was the wisest course in a war, everybody said; avoid entanglements. But as he watched Franny hurrying down the path, buttoning her coat as she ran — a slender, pale-skinned, dark-haired girl with quick almond eyes and a way of sensing your feelings — his heart was in his throat.

He slept badly that night. In the morning, during the exercises over Cape Cod, he went through his duties by rote, filled with misgivings. With the *Shiloh* no longer an abstraction but an unavoidable reality, docked within view of the squadron ready room, he could see that he had never really expected to sail. It amazed him how effectively he had shut out the ultimate purpose of their presence at Quonset Point, as if the war would somehow go away. When the ship's sailing date was posted — December 18 — and all leave and liberty were canceled until further notice, he panicked.

"I won't get to see Franny again," he said to Hildy. "Or my family."

He talked to Commander Scott.

"Relax, Nick," Mr. Scott said. "I just got word that half the squadron will be allowed liberty the weekend before we sail. From five Friday till noon Monday."

"Which duty section, sir?"

"It wouldn't be fair to do it by duty sections," Mr. Scott said. "We're going to draw lots."

The drawing was held two days later. Mr. Scott won; Nick and Hildy lost.

"It's not fair," Nick complained to Franny on the phone. "I've got half a mind to go over the hill."

"Nickie! Don't you dare talk like that. You'd be court-martialed. Talk to Hildy. He'll find a way."

Hildy did. That night, in the barracks, he came by
Nick's bunk with Barney Jacob, the turret gunner on
Ensign Tull's crew. Barney, their closest friend among
the aircrewmen, handed Nick a liberty card.

"I lucked out in the drawing, Nick," he said. "But I
really don't need it."

"But your wife is here visiting," Nick protested.
"With the baby. You need it more than any of us."

"She's leaving Friday. Besides " — Barney looked
around the barracks — "don't tell anyone, but she's been
staying on the base, at Doc Boyd's place over in MOQ."
Lieutenant Boyd was the air group's flight surgeon. "Take
the card, Nick, and go home and see your folks."

Nick hugged Barney and danced with joy — then
abruptly stopped. "That takes care of me," he said to
Hildy. "But what about you?"

Hildy grinned and flashed a second liberty card.

"I bought it off Charlie Wilson for twenty bucks,"
he said. "Charlie's afraid that if he goes ashore, he'll get
beered-up and miss our takeoff."

Barney Jacob's liberty card, Nick soon discovered,
solved one problem and created another: how to divide
the weekend between his family and Franny. Hildy would
go home to Philadelphia with him, of course; there was
no time for a trip to Minnesota. But what about Franny
and Diane?

Hildy came up with the solution. Mr. Scott, he
learned, would be driving down to New York to leave
some personal things at home. He planned to drive back
to Quonset Point on Sunday night and leave his car with
the base operations officer while the *Shiloh* was at sea.

"The four of us are welcome to ride back with him,"
Hildy said.

And so the final scheme was this: Franny and Diane would spend the weekend at Franny's place in New York. Nick and Hildy would come up from Philadelphia on Sunday afternoon. She had also invited Mr. Scott. They would have a late supper and then drive back to Rhode Island.

"Oh, God," Franny said with a sigh after it had all been explained. "I feel as though I'm involved in some conspiracy."

"Will you be able to go down on the train with us Friday?" Nick asked her.

"No. Diane's got a make-up test. We can't leave till Saturday morning. But we'll have plenty of time together on Sunday."

It was a busy week for VT-43 — medical checkups, dental checkups, inoculations, the tedious labeling and packing of the squadron's equipment into wooden chests that would be lashed into the bomb bays of the planes — flight gear, administrative records, survival equipment, hand guns and hunting knives that the crews would carry in combat operations. By Friday afternoon, Nick was an emotional wreck. He put in six calls to Franny but couldn't reach her. At four o'clock, he tried again, from a phone booth outside the Ship's Service Building.

"Where the hell have you *been*?" he said when she came on the line.

"At the library," Franny said. "Back in the stacks. You don't have to be so snotty about it, Nick. After all, life isn't coming to a standstill just because you're shipping out."

"I'm sorry, Franny." He drew a deep breath. "Is everything still okay at your end?"

"Yes. Diane and I are taking a one o'clock train tomorrow. What about you?"

"Yes. Hildy and I are all packed."

"Are you going to talk to your parents? You know,
about us?"

"Yes," Nick said. "What about your father?"

"No. It's too soon. I want you to meet him first. We'll
pretend we're just friends. Agreed?"

"Agreed."

"Are you all right, Nickie?"

"A little edgy, but the trip might help. I need some
time to think."

"Keep remembering how much I love you."

"Oh, God, Franny. That's the only thing that keeps
me going — "

When Nick left the phone booth, retreat was sound-
ing, the bugle call that announced the lowering of the
flag. Automatically, he came to attention and saluted. The
flagpole was in a frozen rock garden in front of the Administration Building. As the colors came down, he felt like
crying. Not out of sentiment or nostalgia, but out of
self-contempt. Partly because of the way he'd behaved all
week, scheming like a spoiled brat to get some time with
Franny and his family, but mostly because of the *Shiloh*
and what awaited him in the Pacific.

He was afraid he was a coward.

3. A LITTLE PIECE OF THE COUNTRY

ALL OVER AMERICA, RAILROAD STATIONS
were great centers of the comings and goings of a nation
at war. Ten million men and women were in uniform,

and more were being called up every day. Relatively few of them could afford the luxury of first-class parlor cars or Pullman sleepers, and even when they could, coach rates were too big a bargain to pass up. Military personnel could buy a round-trip coach ticket at the one-way price. If no return trip was planned — and frequently it wasn't — the unused portion could be cashed in. Nick and Hildy had accumulated a stack of such unused tickets, with which they intended to finance a grand celebration when the war ended.

"Well, two more for our kitty," Nick said as they left the ticket window at Union Station. "I'll ask Franny to keep them for us while we're gone."

Since the arrival of the *Shiloh,* Nick had become increasingly aware of final things. They would probably never see Providence again, certainly not in the same circumstances. Nor would they dance at the casino or drink ale at the little downstairs bar at the Biltmore. And now, as they hurried through the crowded concourse, he remembered the many nights they'd raced to catch the Wickford local.

"It's really not a bad town, is it?" he said to Hildy.

"Providence?" Hildy replied. "It's a swell town. We've had some good times. I'll never forget it."

The seven o'clock train to Philadelphia, which originated in Boston, was twenty minutes late. It was a typical wartime train — drab, outmoded equipment, dirty and overcrowded, with crying babies and a stale smell in the coaches. Nick and Hildy boarded the last car. Three soldiers were passing around a bottle of whiskey in the vestibule. One of them had vomited in a corner.

"The railroads must be making a killing off the war," Nick remarked as they stepped around the mess.

"Everybody's making a killing off the war," Hildy said. "War workers, used-car dealers, butchers."

"What about us?" Nick asked.

"We're making the biggest killing of all." Hildy pushed open the door of the coach and grinned. "We met Diane and Franny, didn't we? And we're getting an expense-paid tour of the Pacific."

"Hildy, sometimes your optimism slays me. You'd probably find redeeming features in Adolph Hitler."

"Could be," Hildy said, and winked. "You know what they say about Mussolini. He made the trains run on time."

They found seats together — briefly. When the train began to move, Hildy noticed a girl standing in the aisle, a baby in her arms and a lost look in her eyes. He nudged Nick.

"The seats are all taken, Nick," he said. "We can't let her stand."

Nick was settling back for a snooze. "I know, I know." He yawned and collected his hat and pea coat. "Sometimes chivalry can be a royal pain."

"That's the whole point, Nick, old boy." Hildy stood up and signaled to the girl. "If it isn't a pain, it isn't chivalry."

They helped the girl fix a bed for the baby in the seat next to the window.

"Thanks loads," she said, smiling with relief. "You can't imagine what it's like, traveling with a baby."

She was a small girl, not more than eighteen years of age, with a bright, eager manner. She came from Petersburg, Illinois, she told them; it was a small town on the Sangamon River. She had been visiting her husband, who was stationed at Quonset Point — with VT-43, it turned out.

"I'll bet you're Barney Jacob's wife," Hildy said.

"You know him!" she exclaimed. "How wonderful!"

"Know him," Nick said. "We're good friends. I understand you stayed with Doc Boyd and his wife, in the married officers' quarters."

"He was so nice," she said. "It was against regulations, but when he found out that I'd brought the baby, he wouldn't hear of a hotel."

They chatted all the way to New York City, with Hildy slouched against an armrest and Nick sitting in the aisle on his seabag, which was stuffed with the dirty skivvies and dungarees, his and Hildy's, that he was taking home to be laundered. The girl — her name was Loretta — spoke of her job in a local drug store; of Barney, who had been two years ahead of her in high school; of her worries about what might happen to him in the Pacific. She and the baby were living with Barney's parents, she said.

"But it's only temporary," she added, a bit proudly. "Barney and I are saving to build a house overlooking the river."

In New London, a vendor came through the coach with snacks and magazines and souvenirs. Hildy treated them to ham sandwiches, milk, and chocolate cake with coconut frosting. By the time they reached Penn Station, where Barney's wife had to change for a Chicago train, they were old friends.

"It's been wonderful meeting you." She bundled up the baby, who was crying, and gave each of them a quick kiss. "God bless you. I feel better about things, knowing that Barney has such good friends."

Nick and Hildy waved to her from the window. She seemed so tiny, so vulnerable, Nick thought, and he hoped everything would work out for her.

"She's a nice girl, isn't she?" Hildy said.

"Yes," Nick answered. "Barney had better take good care of himself."

The train was moving again. Hildy dozed off. Nick tried to sleep but kept remembering Barney Jacob's wife and her anxieties about the war. He had no illusions about combat. The carrier air groups were taking a terrible beating. So many TBFs had been shot down that the plane had been dubbed "the Flying Coffin." And then there were the kamikazes, suicide planes with thousand-pound bombs. Diane was right — how did you fight an enemy who had no will to live? So far, it had all been pretending — the radio and radar training, the gunnery and navigation, the mock torpedo runs out over the Atlantic. Like prep school, in a way. But now . . .

He gazed out the window. The train was speeding through the industrial belt of northern New Jersey. Lights glared from the factories, silhouetting the trains that flashed by in the opposite direction, troop trains, coal trains, trains with tanks and artillery guns lashed to flat-bed freight cars. There was no escaping the war, he thought. Still, there were ways of avoiding combat, angles that could be worked. His family had connections. Or he could claim to be psychologically unfit for flying; the Navy was fussy about the stability of its flight crews. He would be transferred out of aviation, of course, to a line ship, perhaps, or to a shore duty assignment in the Pacific. Which was all right; there were a lot of safe places in combat zones — supply depots, staging areas, communications centers. But how would he face his father, who had fought in France in 1917 and was still bothered by his war wounds? And what about Hildy? He couldn't imagine the Navy without Hildy. They'd been together since

Farragut, the new boot camp in the mountains of Idaho. Hildy had pulled him through the rough spots, both at the technical training center near Memphis and at the air gunners' school in Miami. Nick had almost washed out in Miami, but Hildy had coached him, encouraged him, and when they teamed up with Mr. Scott and began flying, at NAS Fort Lauderdale, they had emerged the top crew.

Red Wing made a difference, he supposed. The aircrewmen from small towns seemed more confident than the others, more flexible. They knew about mechanics and crops and the weather, and were good in emergencies. Nick had visited Red Wing with Hildy after boot camp. He remembered the endless fields of wheat and the sharp Minnesota air. From Hildy's bedroom, you could see the great transcontinental passenger trains racing up the Mississippi River, bound for Portland and Seattle. Hildy loved trains. "One day I'm going to ride the Twentieth Century Limited," he promised his parents. The Hildebrandts lived on High Street, in a white frame house with green shutters. The kitchen smelled of naphtha soap and cinnamon, and there was an apple tree in the backyard. The family seemed to live in the kitchen — Hildy's mother, a slightly plump woman, putting up tomatoes and corn relish; his father, a mailman, soaking his feet at the end of the day; his kid sister, Phoebe, crawling into Hildy's lap with her homework. Everyone in town knew Hildy. In high school, he had lettered in football and track, and when he strolled up Main Street, the merchants called hello. Red Wing would be a good place to get away from the war. Yes. They would go there soon, in the summer, all of them, to the rolling wheat fields . . . Hildy and Diane running on ahead — they were always running —

and he and Franny lingering behind, stretched out deep in the wheat, under the sun, Franny's damp dress clinging to her legs and specks of chaff in her dark hair ... *"Oh, Nickie, I do love you"* ... kissing, touching, pressing ... *"We shouldn't, Nickie. Not here"* ... *"It's all right. No one can see"* ... then her arms coming up around him —

"Wake up, Nick." Hildy was shaking him. "We're coming into Thirtieth Street Station."

Nick sat up and rubbed his eyes. "I was dreaming," he said.

"About what?"

"You'd never guess. Red Wing."

"Red Wing?" Hildy said, surprised. "Maybe after this weekend I'll start dreaming about Rittenhouse Square."

Nick crooned a few bars of a familiar song — "You tell me your dreams, I'll tell you mine" — and they both laughed.

It was snowing in Philadelphia. They hurried to the taxi ramp and hailed a cab. It was nearly two o'clock, and they were both very tired.

"Rittenhouse Square," Nick told the driver, and then to Hildy, "My folks are deep sleepers. I'd just as soon we went right up to bed. Okay?"

"Suits me," Hildy said.

Nick felt nervous about seeing his parents. He hadn't been home since being transferred to Quonset Point, and they knew nothing about Franny. He watched the familiar landmarks slip by in the night — St. Luke's, where he'd made his First Communion, the school on Chestnut Street, with a statue of Benjamin Franklin in the yard. When he caught his first glimpse of the square, his heart quickened, and for a moment it was as if he were coming home from prep school for the holidays. There would be a whirl of parties and a big Christmas dance at the Bellevue-Stratford . . .

"There's the square, Hildy," he said.

Hildy peered through the window and let out a low whistle. "Gosh, Nick," he said. "I knew you lived in a nice neighborhood, but I didn't expect anything like this."

The square was a little park, really, a common, with a fountain and benches and diagonal walks lighted by street lamps with rounded globes, like gaslights. It seemed of another age, the square and the fine old buildings that faced it. The Gothic tower of a church rose above the tall trees. The Enright house was at the foot of the square, opposite the church, in a row of brownstones with wide bay windows and yule wreaths on the doors.

"It's the second house from the corner," Nick told the driver. "The one with the light on."

"I've never been in a three-story house before," Hildy remarked.

"You do a lot of climbing," Nick said. "But it's very private, especially when my sisters are away."

Later, in Nick's third-floor bedroom at the front of the house — after they had tiptoed up the carpeted stairs to avoid waking his parents, Hildy had put on a pair of Nick's pajamas, and Nick was wearing an old wool robe with frayed sleeves, both of them feeling tired but unused to the softness of the beds — they talked.

"Well, Nick," Hildy said, "now that you're home, would you care to talk about it?"

"Talk about what?"

"Whatever it is that's been bothering you."

It was a large, high-ceilinged room, with two beds,

a desk, and a row of bookcases with glass doors. Hildy was lying on the floor; Nick was slouched in a leather armchair next to the window.

"Hildy, you can read me like a book, can't you?" he said, smiling.

"Not always. What's the problem — Franny?"

"No. Combat. I'm scared stiff."

Hildy grinned. "Welcome to the club," he said. "I'll probably fill my pants the first time the Japs shoot at us."

"I'm serious, Hildy. I'm afraid I'll panic and get us all killed. I'm not exactly a marksman with that tail gun, you know."

"You're getting better. Besides, the tail gunner seldom gets a good shot. The main thing is to spray out a lot of tracers and chase the Japs up to me."

"It's no use, Hildy." Nick shook his head doubtfully. "I won't be able to cut it."

"For crying out loud, Nick. You said that at Memphis, and you said it at Miami. Don't worry. You'll cut it."

"But what if I'm too scared to pull the trigger?"

"Don't worry about that tail gun, Nick, You've got plenty of other things to do — the radio and the radar, the arming lever for the torpedo, the oxygen system, changing my ammo can, and holding the relief tube for me when my bladder's bursting — "

"You know what Mr. Scott says," Nick said. "You should take care of those things at the barracks."

They both laughed. Nick was beginning to feel better. It was true, as radioman he did have other responsibilities, and he handled those quite well. He could thread a needle with the radar, Hildy had once said.

"Have you thought much about what might happen to us out there, Hildy?"

"Sure. I've thought about it since the night we saw the *Shiloh* coming up the bay. It's funny about the war, Nick. I was a freshman in high school when the Germans invaded Poland. I really didn't pay much attention to it; it seems there's always a war in Europe. Then, the day before I turned sixteen, the Japs hit Pearl Harbor, and I still wasn't too concerned. It was somebody else's war. I'd never fight in it. And all through training, I felt the same way — that something would come up, that the Japs would surrender, or we'd invent a secret weapon. And so here I am — "

He reached for a pillow and propped it under his head.

"But I'll tell you something, Nick," he went on. "You go to the movies and see John Garfield or Dennis Morgan or somebody fighting for his country, and it's all very thrilling. Sort of silly, but thrilling. Well, I don't know what they're talking about. I've never laid eyes on most of the country and probably never will, so how can I fight for it? But Red Wing is something else. Red Wing is my town. And so I try to picture the Jap armies coming down the Mississippi. Would I fight? You're damn right I would. I'd fight like hell. I might get killed or maimed or end up a basket case, but I'd fight like hell. I think that's how a country gets fought for — in little pieces. For me, it's Red Wing. For Barney Jacob, it's a cute little wife and a house on the Sangamon River. For Mr. Scott, it's probably a few square blocks of Brooklyn Heights — "

"And for me, it's Rittenhouse Square," Nick said. "Is that what you're saying?"

"Well, old buddy, this *is* your neck of the woods."

Nick leaned forward in his chair and looked out the window at the snow falling over the square. He loved the square. He had been wheeled in it when he was a baby; had played leapfrog in it as a child; had held hands with his first date on a bench next to the fountain; and now, scarcely into his manhood, he had come back to it for comfort. His little piece of the country. He knew what the Japanese had done in the Philippines — and in China and Burma and every other country they'd invaded. Unspeakable atrocities. He imagined enemy tanks rumbling down Chestnut Street. Soldiers with bayonets would herd the people into the square and —

Yes, he would fight for it. He would die for it.

"Hildy," he said, "you're a regular sage." He yawned and gave his friend a little kick. "Come on, let's get some sleep."

4. So Solid, So Enduring

THEY SLEPT TILL TEN, AT WHICH TIME THE bedroom door flew open, the window shades clattered up, and Margaret Enright, a large, vigorous woman with firm ways, burst upon them — with hugs and kisses for Nick and a warm handshake for Hildy, who wasn't quite awake.

"You're what I'd expect of Minnesota, Hildy — blond all over," she said, and then to her son, who was reaching for his robe, "Nick, must you wear that threadbare garment?"

Nick's father, George Enright, watched from the doorway, smiling. A pleasant man, who smoked a pipe and wore vested suits, he looked like what he was — a Philadelphia lawyer, a senior partner of an old and respected Broad Street firm.

"Well, boys," he said, crossing the room to greet them, "this time it certainly looks like the Pacific."

"I guess so, Dad," Nick said, warmly embracing his father. "This is no drill, as they say on the poop deck."

"Nick!" his mother said. "Such language."

"There's nothing wrong with it, Mother. At the stern of certain Naval vessels there's a deck called the poo——"

"Never mind." Margaret Enright busied herself with the contents of Nick's seabag. "Good grief, you've got a ton of dirty clothes."

"Hildy's things are in there, too," Nick said. "In the small bundle."

"I'll call Mr. Cheng at the laundry," his mother said. "He'll have them back by five. I've still got some of your name tags from Saint Crispin's," she added. "I'll ask Mr. Cheng to sew them in."

"But, Mother," Nick protested. "We've got stencils for that. With our name, rate, and serial number."

"Stencils? And smear your clothes with ink? You're going to have civilized name tags, young man, Navy or no Navy."

Nick appealed to his father. "Dad, will you please explain to her — "

"Not now, Nick," George Enright replied, and amiably steered his wife to the door. "We'd better let them get dressed, Margaret. Breakfast is on the stove, boys" he called back. "Scrapple and eggs. And then let's have a talk, Nick. In the library."

The library, a comfortable room paneled in oak, was George Enright's retreat, off limits to others except by invitation. Nick was always pleased when his father asked to see him there.

"I hope Hildy won't think you're neglecting him,"

George Enright said as they settled into wing chairs near the window.

"He's upstairs listening to my Glenn Miller records," Nick said. "He's a great Miller fan. He might be there all day."

"I'm afraid there won't be time," his father said. "Has your mother told you the schedule?"

"Not yet."

"We're having an early Christmas — for you and Hildy. Pity your sisters couldn't get home from school, but they'll have their celebration next week. So just pretend that today is Christmas Eve. We'll trim the tree tonight, and then have a big turkey dinner tomorrow."

"Gosh, Dad," Nick said. "Mother shouldn't have gone to all that trouble. Just being home is enough."

"I know," his father replied, lighting his pipe. "But she wanted it that way. You'll have to make allowances for her, Nick. It isn't every day her only son ships out for the Pacific."

"I know, Dad," Nick said. "But sometimes I just don't understand her. She acts as if I'm going off to summer camp or someplace. All that fuss about name tags and laundry — "

"It's her way of managing, Nick, to pretend that threatening situations don't exist. This isn't her first war, remember."

The room was lined with books and law volumes, save for the wall behind George Enright's desk, which was reserved for memorabilia — photographs, diplomas, citations from various bar associations. Nick's eyes fell on the yellowed picture of his father's Army company, taken at Fort Dix in 1917.

"How old were you when your outfit was sent overseas, Dad?" he asked.

"Twenty." His father turned in his chair and looked up at the photograph. "It seems ancient history now, but it was only twenty-six — no, twenty-seven — years ago. We marched up Fifth Avenue in New York. There was confetti and a brass band. Your mother was there."

"Really?" Nick said. "I didn't know that."

"Oh, yes. She waved to me from the curb. She was wearing one of those sailor-type dresses that were in fashion back then."

"Mother in a sailor-suit dress?" Nick laughed. "I don't believe it."

"Oh, your mother had her day, Nick. She was at the dock when we sailed, and when they shipped me back from France, she came to the hospital every day. Military hospitals are tragic places during a war. She saw many gruesome things. Yes, she knows about war . . ."

Nick hoped his father would tell him more about the Great War, but George Enright fell into silence.

"Dad," Nick said after a moment, "I know you were in the trenches over there, but I've never heard you talk about it."

"No, and you probably never will." He reached for an ashtray and tapped the ashes from his pipe. "Combat sets you apart, Nick. You can talk about it only with men who have experienced it."

"Do you ever see any of your old Army buddies?"

"Occasionally. Four or five of us get together now and then. We have a few drinks and reminisce. There's not much to remember, really. The camaraderie and the horror. In the end, that's all you're left with. Camaraderie . . . horror . . ." He gave an embarrassed laugh and looked at his watch. "Shouldn't you look in on Hildy?"

"In a minute, Dad," Nick said. "There's something

else, something that might upset Mother." He drew a deep breath. "I've met a girl."

"Good." His father smiled. "What's so upsetting about that?"

"She's Jewish."

"Oh-h," George Enright said in a low voice.

Nick told him the whole story — about Franny, about the reception at Wickford, about Diane and Hildy.

"She's from New York, you say?"

"Yes, sir. Her father's a physician, a fairly prominent neurologist, apparently."

"Not Saul Kaplan."

"Yes, that's him. Why?"

"He's one of the top men in his field. Our firm has called on him in several major accident suits."

"You mean you've met him?" Nick asked, surprised.

"Of course. Haven't you?"

"No, sir. I'll meet him tomorrow. We're stopping at Franny's on the way back. What kind of person is he?"

"I haven't spent much time with him, Nick. But I'd say Saul Kaplan is as fine a man as you and I will ever meet."

He shook his head in disbelief.

"Nick Enright and Saul Kaplan's daughter," he said. "Who would have believed it? I won't deny you've opened a real can of worms, Nick. But we'll just put the matter on the back burner for now. The immediate item of business is to get you through the war in one piece."

"Thanks, Dad."

"Don't be so quick with your thanks, Nick. You're facing problems you can't begin to imagine. Your family, her family, the reaction of friends — "

"What's your reaction, Dad? Do you object?"

"Object? How could I possibly object? If you're old enough to go to war, you're certainly old enough to determine your personal relationships without family interference. But let me ask you this." He leaned back in his chair and gave his son a long look. "We live with our decisions, Nick. From the cradle to the grave, life is a continuity of decisions. Boyhood, adolescence, middle age — there are no clean slates. Decisions made in our youth bind us as adults. The divorce courts are filled with people who weren't prepared to live with their decisions. So — what I'm leading up to is this. Are you prepared to live with yours?"

Nick suddenly felt nervous. His father had a way of reducing things to fundamentals. He got to his feet and paced the floor for a few moments. He was wearing gray flannel slacks and his old St. Crispin's blazer. He wished he'd worn his dress blues instead. He felt oddly uncomfortable out of uniform, oddly immature.

"Civilian clothes don't feel right anymore," he said. "Was it that way with you, Dad?"

"Yes." His father smiled. "It took me months to get used to them again."

Nick looked out the window. It was snowing again. In the square, workmen were stringing colored lights on the annual Christmas tree. Two boys were making a snowman, using pieces of coal for the face. Watching them, Nick imagined married life with Franny. A continuity of decisions, his father had said. They could handle the religious complications; he was confident of that. But the children — how would they be raised? Catholic? Jewish? In his mind, he could resolve every difficulty but that one. But, he and Franny together — who could say what novel arrangements they might come up with?

"Yes, Dad," he finally answered. "I'm prepared."

"Then the die is cast, as Caesar said." George Enright stood up and shook hands with his son. "Don't worry about your mother, Nick. I'll do some spadework in that area while you're gone. But I think it's up to you to inform her that Franny is, shall we say, of a different faith."

"Yes, sir," Nick replied. "I'll try not to hurt her."

"Fine." His father gave him an encouraging slap on the back. "Now you'd better see to your house guest."

When Nick got up to his room, Hildy was lying on the floor, listening to "Moonlight Serenade."

"How did it go with your dad, Nick?" he asked, turning off the phonograph.

"It went fine," he replied. "Just fine." And then, unaccountably, his eyes filled with tears. "My father's a great guy, Hildy. A really great guy."

That afternoon, Nick took Hildy sightseeing, to Independence Hall and the Betsy Ross House — by street car, inasmuch as George Enright had used up his gasoline ration coupons for the month. Afterward, they went Christmas shopping, at Wanamaker's, the big department store on Market Street. Nick had paid little attention to the forthcoming holidays, but now he found himself succumbing to the Christmas mood of the city. It was pleasant, he thought, mingling with the shoppers and browsing through the fine old store, the aisles decorated with holly and mistletoe, and the department store chimes ringing softly in the background, like notes struck on a xylophone. Even with the many wartime shortages, the display cases glittered with an abundance of merchandise — candies, electric trains, fine millinery, even imported figurines. Hildy couldn't resist a comparison. "I wonder

what the Christmas shopping is like in Berlin this year."
On the mezzanine, they stopped at the tobacco counter.
"What brand does your dad smoke, Nick?" Nick suggested cigars instead. "He always has plenty of tobacco,
but he likes a cigar after dinner." Hildy chose a box of
perfectos; on the fourth floor, near the linens department,
he spotted a box of small linen guest towels in pastel colors. Nick said, "That's just the kind of thing my mother
would choose herself." And that evening, when Margaret
Enright opened the gift, she smiled with unfeigned en-
thusiasm. "Hildy, this is exactly the kind of hand towel
I like for my house."

Nick had worried about how his mother would react
to Hildy. He needn't have. She had warmed to him from
the start, and he won her over completely at dinner by
his honest bewilderment at the sight of all the silverware.
When he stared at the profusion of spoons and knives
and forks, Nick knew what he was going through in his
mind. In Red Wing, meals were served in the kitchen,
with a bottle of milk on the table and toast crumbs in the
butter dish.

"Golly, Mrs. Enright," Hildy said, "there're so many,
I don't know which spoon to pick up."

Whereupon Margaret Enright launched into a lesson
on table etiquette. "You always start with the outermost
utensil. When you've finished your fruit cup, you know,
of course, to place the spoon on the saucer and not leave
it in the cup. And — "

"Margaret," her husband said gently, "perhaps
you're embarrassing Hildy."

"Oh, no, Mrs. Enright," Hildy said. "I'm really interested."

"Of course he is, George," Margaret Enright said.

"Besides, he'll be joining an eating club at Princeton, and they'll expect him to know such things."

"Princeton?" Hildy said, and swallowed a mouthful of fruit in a gulp. "Me?"

"But you'll be coming east to college after the war, won't you? You and Nick have been such good friends, you'll want to stay together."

"Gosh, Mrs. Enright, my father is just a mailman. I doubt if he could even afford to send me to the state university in Minneapolis."

"You're overlooking something, Hildy," Nick said. "Congress just passed the GI Bill. The government will pay for it."

"Hey, that's right," Hildy said in a whisper. "I completely forgot."

"Five hundred a year for tuition," Nick said, "and fifty a month for living expenses."

Hildy began to grasp the possibilities.

"Boy, would my dad be proud," he said, his blue eyes glowing. "His son at an Ivy League college."

"Well, how about it?" Nick said, pressing him. "Dad's on one of the alumni committees. He'll see that you get an application form."

"I can't imagine a school like that accepting me," Hildy said. "But . . . okay."

Nick was ebullient. "Swell, Hildy," he said, shaking his friend's hand. "We'll be sticking together."

"This calls for a toast," George Enright said. "Margaret, there's a bottle of champagne chilling outside in the milk box. I was saving it for tomorrow," he added to the boys, "but it isn't every day that a friend of Nick's from Minnesota decides to apply to Princeton."

Margaret Enright brought out her best crystal.

"Nick, do you want to do the honors?" his father asked.

"You do it, Dad. You're better with words."

They stood and raised their glasses.

"To Hildy and Nick," George Enright said. "Friends, shipmates, future classmates. May the Lord bless them and keep them, all the days of their lives."

The next afternoon, after Mass at St. Luke's, which Hildy attended with the family, and a big Christmas dinner, with chestnut stuffing and three kinds of dessert, it was time to leave. Margaret Enright had put in calls to Nick's sisters in Northfield and to Red Wing, but the circuits to Minnesota were busy, and the call didn't come through until George Enright was helping Nick and Hildy carry their bags to the vestibule.

"Hurry, Hildy!" Margaret Enright called to him. "It's your mother!"

Everybody talked to everybody. "Yes, he looks fine, Mrs. Hildebrandt," Margaret Enright said when it was her turn. "We fattened him up a bit. Now if you and Mr. Hildebrandt ever come to Philadelphia, please plan to stay with us. We have plenty of room, and we'd love to have you . . ."

"The taxi's here!" George Enright called from the front window.

Nick put his arm around his mother and walked with her to the door.

"Honestly, Nick, I don't see why you can't take a later train," she said. "Exactly who is this girl you're seeing in New York?"

"Frances Kaplan," Nick replied. "She goes to Wickford."

"Chapman? Your father knows a Chapman on Fifth Avenue."

"Kaplan, Mother," Nick repeated. "With a *K*. Franny is Jewish."

"Jewish?" Margaret Enright put a hand to her mouth. "Oh, dear," she said in a weak voice.

And then George Enright was herding them all through the vestibule and down the front steps. There was a rush of anxious good-bys and nervous laughter. "Take good care of yourself, son." "I will, Dad. And thanks for everything." "Oh, dear God, Nickie, I can't believe you're going." "I'll be fine, mother. The *Shiloh* is a good ship, and Mr. Scott is a great pilot." And then the cab drove off.

"They're terrific people, Nick," Hildy said, waving through the rear window. "I wouldn't have missed this weekend for anything."

It had been a good visit, Nick thought; the best he could remember. He felt very hopeful. In a few hours, he would be seeing Franny again. They would have the evening together, and then the long drive to Rhode Island. It was turning out to be a good farewell.

"That was pretty clever of you, Nick," Hildy said, "the way you slipped Franny to your mother."

"Yes," Nick agreed, smiling. "I thought so, too."

As the cab turned away from the square, he looked back. His mother and father were waving from the curb. He rolled down a window and waved with his hat. They looked so solid, so enduring. He hated leaving them, knowing how they would study the war news in the papers and hold their breath every time they saw a Western Union boy nearby. But he would be back soon, he and Hildy, safe and whole. He was sure of it.

5. WINE AND CROSSES

BEING IN THE NAVY HAD INVOLVED DIFFI-
cult adjustments for Nick, whose background of boarding
schools and summers at Cape May had poorly equipped
him for the less congenial aspects of military life — the
harsh discipline, the five A.M. calisthenics, the constant
lack of privacy. As a recruit, he had become seriously con-
stipated before he could bring himself to use the com-
munal toilet facilities — the "head" — where the stalls
had no doors. And he was stunned by the language of
some of his shipmates, who seemed to communicate ex-
clusively in four-letter expletives. He felt himself an outsider, unable to fit in, and yearned for home.

Then one night at Farragut, the training base on
Lake Pend Oreille in northern Idaho, he woke from a
troubled sleep and heard the boy in the bunk below him
sobbing into his pillow. *"Mama, Mama."* The boy was
from Salinas, California, of Mexican parentage. Nick
didn't like him; he was a braggart and had vulgar habits.
But lying sleepless in the darkened barracks, listening to
the boy's muffled sobs and wondering what the future
held, Nick realized that they were both in the same boat,
whatever their habits, sharing the same fears and uncertainties, the same loneliness. The next day, the Mexican
boy was transferred to an outgoing unit. (Later, Nick
would learn that he'd been eaten by sharks when the
Samuel B. Roberts, a destroyer, went down in the Philippine Sea.) That afternoon, Hildy moved into the lower
bunk, and Nick's life began to change.

"I've found out why the Navy put a boot camp way

up here in the wilderness," Hildy said as they introduced themselves.

"Really?" Nick said, a bit suspiciously. "Why?"

Hildy grinned. "It was Mrs. Roosevelt's fault," he said. "She was in Spokane making a speech and flew over Lake Pend Oreille on her way back to the White House. 'My, what a lovely lake,' she said. 'I must tell Franklin to build a Naval base there.'"

That was Hildy, making the most of things. They became inseparable friends, arranging to sit together at chow, march together in drill formation, even scrub decks together. When Nick had difficulty qualifying on the rifle range, Hildy pulled him through.

"Don't jerk the trigger, Nick. Squeeze it. Pretend it's a sponge."

Through Hildy's influence, Nick slowly came to terms with the Navy, discovering admirable traits in others, and in himself, abilities he'd never known he possessed — until he reached the painful conclusion that, despite its many advantages, his background had really been quite limited, a tight little world of privilege and Roman Catholic tradition that had shut him off from much of life . . .

And now, in a taxi in New York City — the cab turning into Seventy-first Street and nearly getting stuck in the snow, which was coming down heavily, Hildy gawking at the tall buildings and Nick fiddling with the box of Schrafft's chocolates they'd bought at Penn Station — Nick felt the same misgivings he'd had in boot camp. This would be his first visit to a Jewish household, and he cursed the narrowness of his experience. Would he say the right thing? Do the right thing?

"Nervous?" Hildy asked him.

"Yes," he replied. "Does it show?"

"No, you look fine," Hildy said. "Here, let me straighten your neckerchief."

The Kaplans' apartment was on the eighteenth floor of a building just off Park Avenue. They left their bags with the doorman, who directed them to the elevators. Nick felt his anxiety mounting, but the moment Franny opened the door, wearing a ruffled apron over her sweater and skirt, his misgivings left him. There was an immediate aura of warm family life — the smell of baking, a wall of bookcases to one side, the clutter of galoshes and forgotten hockey sticks in the foyer closet.

"Mr. Scott is already here," Franny told them as she took their coats. "He thinks we shouldn't start back until it stops snowing. It might be an all-night drive."

"Fine," Nick said. "I'd hate to waste our last night in the barracks."

"It's like prom night, Franny," Hildy added. "Who wants to sleep?"

Nick heard Diane's laughter coming from the living room, and then she was rushing out to greet them, followed by Mr. Scott, who was wearing aviation greens, and Franny's father. Dr. Kaplan was a small man with ramrod-straight posture and, behind gold-rimmed glasses, brown eyes like Franny's. His crisp white shirt looked as if it had just come out of the box.

"Let me see" — he smiled and gripped Nick's hand firmly — "you must be Nick."

"Yes, sir," Nick replied, and it occurred to him that if he were a patient, he would have complete trust in this man. "And this is Hildy, our turret gunner."

"Oh, I've heard all about Hildy from Diane," Dr. Kaplan said. "I'm even familiar with his home town. My work sometimes takes me to the Mayo Clinic, which isn't far from Red Wing."

He chatted about Minnesota and the new burn salve developed at the famous clinic, a kind of tannic acid jelly, which was being used by the Navy. Then he turned back to Nick.

"Nick Enright," he said, studying him more closely. "You wouldn't happen to be George Enright's son, would you?"

"Yes, sir," Nick said, feeling a surge of pride. "My father told me the two of you had met. He spoke very highly of you."

"I consider that an excellent report, coming from George Enright," Dr. Kaplan said, and led them into the living room. "Life is full of coincidences, isn't it? Here we've only just met, and we already know that we have things in common. I was telling Commander Scott that I once lived not far from his home in Brooklyn Heights, in a flat near the bridge, on the wrong side of the tracks, so to speak. My family was very poor, but we had good times, and I still enjoy a stroll in the old neighborhood now and then."

The living room was like the rest of the apartment, from what Nick could see. It was gracious but unpretentious, with a baby grand piano and more bookcases. Sections of the Sunday *Times* lay beside the sofa, and a menorah with lighted Hannukah candles stood on a round mahogany table. The room was large, made even more spacious by the long windows facing south, which offered a lovely view of the snow falling over Manhattan in the early evening light. Nick noticed a big National Geographic map spread out on the floor at one end of the room.

"Commander Scott was about to give us a report on the war in the Pacific when you arrived," Dr. Kaplan explained to Nick and Hildy. He pulled a cushion from the sofa and settled himself on the floor. "Franny, perhaps some wine for our guests."

Franny turned to Nick. "Are you any good with a corkscrew?" she asked politely.

"Yes," Nick replied, remembering their agreement and trying not to appear anxious. "Very good."

In the kitchen, which was through the dining room, Franny waited till the swinging door closed behind Nick and then went into his arms.

"Oh, God, Nickie, I've thought about you all weekend."

"I know." Nick held her close and ran his fingers through her hair. "We've grown on each other, haven't we?"

"Oh, yes, yes, yes. I don't know what I'll do when you're gone."

"It won't be too bad. There'll be letters."

"I wish we'd slept together. At least we'd have that."

"Maybe not. It would ruin everything if your brothers thought I'd been taking you to cheap hotels."

"I suppose you're right." She gave a deep sigh. "Did you talk to your parents?"

"Just my dad. It went better than I expected, and he's going to discuss it with my mother while I'm away. She only knows you exist. What about your father?"

"He senses something between us. I can tell."

"Has he said anything?"

"No. And he won't until I bring it up. That's the way he is. I nearly fell over when he mentioned your father. I had no idea they'd met."

"Neither did I. Do you think it helps?"

"It can't hurt. At least it establishes your credentials — and mine with your family."

"Maybe if we — "

Franny pressed a finger to his lips.

"Please, let's put it aside for now, Nickie," she said. "You've got more important things to worry about. How is your morale?"

"As good as it'll ever be. I had a long talk with Hildy. It helped a lot."

"My compliments to Hildy." Franny smiled. "How did we manage to function before him?"

"It wasn't easy." Nick brushed a tear from her cheek and kissed her lightly on the lips. "Come on, let's get busy with the corkscrew before your father suspects the worst."

It was an evening like fine wine, Nick thought — warm and felicitous. Conversation at the Kaplans' was always stimulating, never frivolous; Franny's father had a way of drawing out the best in his guests. And while they sat around the big map of the Pacific listening to Mr. Scott, his tunic unbuttoned and his gold aviator's wings glittering the light of a tole lamp, Nick kept remembering his talk with Hildy.

" — You mean if we'd lost the Battle of Midway," Diane was saying as Franny passed the wine, "the Japanese would have invaded the United States?"

"Look at the map, Diane." Mr. Scott pointed to the absence of any land masses, and therefore any U.S. military bases, between Midway Island and the American mainland. "With Midway as a staging area, they would have had a clear shot at California."

"Would they have succeeded?" Dr. Kaplan asked.

"What would have stopped them? The Navy? We'd

lost half the Pacific Fleet at Pearl Harbor. The Army? We had none to speak of. The National Guard was conducting training maneuvers with sticks for guns and sacks of flour for bombs. The Japs, on the other hand, had been preparing for war for years. They envisioned an empire that would embrace half the world. They enjoyed overwhelming numerical superiority — in men, planes, ships, tanks, everything. Their strategy was to strike quickly and decisively before we could mobilize and gear up our industrial production. Yes, sir, I think they would have succeeded."

There was a long silence.

"It's scary," Franny said, shivering. "To think we came that close to being invaded."

Dr. Kaplan sipped his wine thoughtfully. "I'm reminded of Churchill's remark about the Spitfire pilots after the London blitz," he said. "About so many owing so much to so few."

"Did the *Shiloh* fight at Midway?" Diane asked.

"Oh, yes," Mr. Scott replied. "The Japanese lost four of their best aircraft carriers. The *Shiloh*'s air group accounted for two of them."

"Did they lose many planes?" she said.

"The bombing squadron put up thirty-four Dauntless dive bombers. Fourteen were shot down."

"And the torpedo squadron?"

"They ran into trouble," Mr. Scott said. "They put up fifteen planes and lost ten."

"Ten out of fifteen!" Diane exclaimed. "That many?"

"Relax, Diane," Hildy said quickly. "That was over two years ago. They were flying the old TBD Devastator. The TBF is a much better plane."

"And the Japanese have probably got better guns,"

she said — and Nick noticed an odd look in Hildy's eyes, as though he were seeing Diane in a new way.

Franny exchanged a meaningful glance with her father, who tactfully folded the map and announced that an informal supper was ready.

"Franny has a buffet waiting for us in the dining room," he said. "Just heap your plates and find a place at the table."

The buffet was spread out on the sideboard.

"Holy cow, Franny, it's a regular picnic," Hildy said, sampling the appetizers — deviled eggs and chopped liver and lox on rounds of dark bread.

There was a platter of corned beef and another of sliced white chicken, with cole slaw and round crusty rolls and rye bread. Franny kept their glasses filled with wine, a prewar Chablis, and as they ate and talked — about books, about schools, about the new Broadway plays — Nick found himself wishing the evening would never end. Dr. Kaplan, who had served in the Vladivostok expedition at the end of World War I, kept them entertained with funny stories about the Army.

"At Camp Kilmer," he said, "I told them I was a medical student, so they assigned me to the motor pool, which is how I ended up a kitchen corporal."

For dessert, there was a choice of honey cake or apple pie.

"I think I'll have both," Hildy said. "And is there any of that smoked salmon left?"

Dr. Kaplan roared with laughter. "Hildy, you're a marvel," he said. "Franny, pack a lunch to take with you. This boy's apt to perish before you reach the Connecticut line."

Diane cleared the dishes while Franny served coffee

and passed around the box of chocolates that Nick and Hildy had brought.

"I just looked out the window," she said. "It's stopped snowing."

Mr. Scott had been holding back on the wine, knowing he had a long drive ahead of him. Now he looked at his watch. "It's after eleven," he said. "We'd better leave by midnight."

Diane whispered something to Franny.

"Oh, my gosh, I nearly forgot," Franny said. "It's in my room." She wiggled a finger at Nick. "I need two strong arms, Nick. Would you mind?"

The bedrooms were down a long hallway off the foyer.

"I really don't need any help," Franny said. "I just wanted to show you something."

She led him into her father's room and opened the closet door.

"My mother's," she said, pointing to the dresses that hung there. "Everything's just as she left it. Even the personal articles on the dresser. My father can't bear to part with them."

"Your parents must have been very close," Nick said.

"Their families came over on the same boat. They were just children then."

"How did she die?"

"A stroke. She'd never been ill a day in her life." She closed the closet door. "It was as though the world had ended."

Franny's room was across the hall. Two overnight bags were on the bed, already packed, and a long package in holiday wrapping. The room was filled with books — on the desk, on chairs, stacked on the floor.

"You can expect me to do a lot of reading in bed."
She smiled demurely and kissed him on the cheek.

Nick carried the overnight bags out to the foyer;
Franny took the package to the dining room and handed
it to Diane, who in turn presented it to Mr. Scott.

"It's a Christmas present," she said with a wide smile.
"It's for all of you, but I think Mr. Scott should open it."

Mr. Scott removed the wrapping and found a cardboard tube containing the Raspberry One insignia Diane
had promised, in the form of a decal that could be bonded
to an airplane.

"The insignia!" he said, completely surprised. "I'd
forgotten all about it."

"I took the artwork to a lithographer in Providence," Diane said. "He suggested the decal."

It was a deceptively simple design — a stylized red
raspberry on a field of green, with *ONE* superimposed in
white. The raspberry was done in slight forward angles
that suggested speed. The effect was that of reluctant
power, as though the artist was expressing the purpose of
the plane and the crew that flew it.

"Well?" Diane said anxiously.

"It's perfect, Diane," Mr. Scott said, and gave her a
warm hug. "We'll be proud to fly with your insignia."

Dr. Kaplan tapped his glass with a spoon. "Speech!"
he called out. "Speech!"

Mr. Scott moved to one end of the table and smiled
shyly.

"Well," he began. "I didn't bring any chocolates, but
I didn't come empty-handed either. Franny, if you'll get
that little carton I left in the foyer — "

Franny brought the box; it contained a wooden
model of a TBF, mounted on a swivel.

"I'm afraid this isn't a very good day for speech-making," Mr. Scott went on. "If you read the *Times* to-day, you know that our armies in Europe are bogged down in Belgium, and between kamikazes and typhoons, I guess we've been losing a lot of ships out in the Pacific. But island by island, we're approaching the ultimate goal of the Pacific campaign — the invasion of Japan. We've come a long way — from Midway to the Philippines — but there's still a long way to go. Which is one of the many reasons we're so grateful to you — Dr. Kaplan, Franny, Diane. Your hospitality has warmed our hearts, and the memory of it will comfort us in the difficult months ahead."

He handed the model TBF to Dr. Kaplan, and continued.

"It seems an inadequate expression of our appreciation, Doctor. But perhaps it will remind you of the pleasant hours we've shared, and encourage you to remember us in your prayers. Thank you again."

Franny was deeply moved. "What a marvelous man," she whispered to Nick. "I'm so glad he's your pilot."

And then it was Dr. Kaplan's turn.

"If I may propose a toast," he said, rising.

The others gathered around him with raised glasses.

"To Raspberry One and the men who fly her — Nick, Hildy, Commander Scott. Godspeed."

It was the second toast of that day, and Nick suddenly felt a grim sense of continuity with his father, with Dr. Kaplan, with all the men who had marched up Fifth Avenue in 1917. The lines of a poem flashed through his mind, a poem he'd studied at St. Crispin's, about the crosses, row on row, in Flanders fields. He reached for

Franny's hand and held it tight, not caring whether her
father noticed.

> To you from failing hands we throw
>   The torch; be yours to hold it high.

He was indeed going off to war.

6. "HELLO, MOTHER GOOSE"

AND THEN THE LONG DRIVE BACK — IN MR.
Scott's 1940 La Salle, a convertible coupe with red leather
upholstery, the car cold and drafty at first, then warm
and snug when the heater started working, Nick and
Franny bundled up in the narrow rear seat, Hildy in
front with his arm around Diane, the tires making a
muffled sound in the snow, across the Bronx, then up the
Boston Post Road, through Rye and Port Chester and
into Connecticut, where it began to snow again.

"Thirty-five is the best we can do in this weather,"
Mr. Scott said. "Diane, what time do you and Franny
have to sign in?"

"There's no rush," she replied. "As long as we make
our eight o'clock class."

Diane turned on the radio and found some music, a
dance orchestra broadcasting from a hotel in Chicago. It
was very pleasant, Nick thought, driving up the Post
Road in the snow and listening to the music, the wind-
shield wipers clicking softly and Franny's head resting on
his shoulder. He thought perhaps he should try to nap,

but he didn't want to waste these last hours with Franny. Besides, there would be time to sleep at Quonset Point. The *Shiloh* wouldn't sail until noon; the air group would take off two hours later and rendezvous with the ship off Connecticut. In his mind, he was already making the transition to the Pacific, eager to get it over with and pick up his life.

"A penny for your thoughts," Franny whispered in his ear.

"That's easy. The *Shiloh*."

"You aren't worried, are you?"

"Not anymore."

"I kept watching you tonight."

"I know. I was watching you."

"I think the weekend was good for you. You seem refreshed."

"Regenerated would be more accurate."

"My father likes you. Did you notice how he put you first in his toast?"

"Yes, but I thought it was just a random thing."

"He never does anything at random."

"Damn it, Franny, I hate leaving you with the situation unresolved."

"But it is resolved." She took his hand and slipped it inside her coat. "Just keep remembering how much I love you . . . Oh, Nickie, I'll miss your hands . . ."

They drove all night. No one said very much; it was enough just to be together. In New Haven, they got stuck in the snow, and Nick and Hildy had to get out and push. They stopped in Old Saybrook for gas, at Al's Always Open, and again at an all-night diner in New London, where they got carry-out coffee to drink with the snacks that Franny had brought along. Dawn was breaking as they crossed into Rhode Island. Diane tuned in a farm program, and then the news came on. There was a story about a German counterattack in Belgium. The 101st Airborne was trapped in Bastogne, and bad weather was preventing the relief of the division by air. Then:

> This just in from London. A plane carrying Major Glenn Miller from London to France, where his Air Corps orchestra was to entertain troops at the battle front, has crashed in the English Channel. Miller, America's most popular orchestra leader before joining the Army two years ago, is presumed dead.

Mr. Scott pounded the steering wheel with his fist. "What rotten luck," he said, almost angrily. "What absolutely rotten luck."

They fell into a stunned silence. They had grown up to Glenn Miller's music. Diane was the first to speak.

"I saw him one summer in the Poconos," she said. "There was a pavilion strung with colored lanterns. It was so lovely."

Diane began crying. "I'll bet it's all a mistake," she said. "Band leaders don't get killed in a war. He's probably floating in a raft somewhere."

Nick felt a sinking sensation in his stomach. The war was producing horrors beyond his comprehension. Russian civilians had eaten the paste off wallpaper in the siege of Stalingrad. There were rumors that Jews were being put to death in gas chambers in German concentration camps. The Japanese had hung American prisoners by the thumbs and stripped their flesh, slice by slice, just for amusement. The death of an orchestra leader he'd never set eyes on shouldn't have bothered him, but it did.

It was nearly eight o'clock when they arrived at Wickford. The driveway into the campus hadn't been plowed. Mr. Scott pulled up at a spot in the road where the snowdrifts weren't too deep. There was no time for lingering farewells — a few kisses, a few tears, and then Franny and Diane were hurrying through the snow, in boots and knee socks and knitted hats pulled down over their ears.

"I just remembered," Franny called back. "We don't have your new address."

"Fleet Post Office, San Francisco," Nick hollered to her. "You're supposed to use V-mail forms."

Nick and Hildy watched till the girls disappeared into the Humanities Building. Then Hildy, predictably, had the last word.

"Well, Nick, you said it yourself. You can always tell a Wickford girl by her knee socks."

The girls had promised to watch for the squadron's takeoff, but the heavy weather hadn't lifted, and if they were at the Point, Nick couldn't see them. The squadron took off precisely on schedule. Snow squalls gusted across the runway, and ice formed briefly on the wings as they climbed to eight thousand feet. Clouds covered the coastline solidly, except for a patch of Connecticut, which was Nick's last glimpse of land. Fifty miles out, the sky was clear. He turned on the radar and quickly picked up six blips, the *Shiloh* and her five escort vessels — two heavy cruisers and three destroyers.

NICK: I have the *Shiloh* on my scope, Skipper. Bearing: five degrees port. Range: four-five miles.

MR. SCOTT: Roger, Nick. See if you can raise them on the horn.

Nick switched the selector on his radio jackbox from the intercom system to the VHF transmitter. Then, nervously, as though making a performing debut, he cleared his throat and pressed his mike button.

NICK: Hello, Mother Goose. Hello, Mother Goose. This is Raspberry One, four-five miles northwest at angels eight, with sixteen — that's one-six — turkeys for landing. Over.

And then he heard for the first time a well-modulated, reassuring voice that would become an important part of his life, although he would never meet the man to whom it belonged.

MOTHER GOOSE: Roger, Raspberry One. This is Mother Goose. We have you on our scope. Descend to angels two and call when you have visual contact. The management and staff welcome you to the *Shiloh*. Happy landing. Out.

It was cold in the plane. Nick blew on his fingers to keep them warm. Four days later, however, when the *Shiloh* was moving through the Panama Canal and he and Hildy were lolling in the sun, stripped to the waist, he had the beginnings of a fine tan.

Franny was never out of his mind.

PART TWO: THE PACIFIC

7. HONING THE EDGE

THE COMMANDING OFFICER OF THE U.S.S. *Shiloh*, Captain Buford G. Rawlins (Annapolis '22), was a robust, outspoken man from Mobile, Alabama, whose Southern accent softened his gruff manner of speaking. Behind his back, he was known as "Iron Gut," a nickname deriving from his service, in 1942, as air officer of the *Hornet*. In the Battle of Santa Cruz, east of the Solomon Islands, he had been caught in an explosion that showered the bridge with slivers of shrapnel. Over a hundred of them peppered his belly, like birdshot. Despite his wounds, he had stubbornly remained at his post until dragged, literally, to a battle dressing station. Captain Rawlins ran a tight ship. His welcoming remarks to VT-43, delivered during a brisk visit to the squadron ready room, were brief and to the point.

"The taxpayers paid a heap of money for the airplanes y'all been sportin' around in," he said, chewing on a cigar. "And you'd better give 'em good value, or I'll radio Admiral Lawton for a batch of replacements."

Captain Rawlins's concept of value, it soon became clear, meant work. Hard work, precise work, unrelenting work. As the *Shiloh* and her escorts steamed northwest across the Pacific, the ship was set at combat readiness. Battle drills around the clock, reconnaissance flights from dawn to dusk, followed by long hours of background

briefings on every aspect of combat operations. What to
do if shot down behind enemy lines. Techniques for
ditching at sea. The use of antishark chemicals. And
every night, aircraft recognition practice, in which sil-
houettes of enemy planes were flashed on a screen for a
twentieth of a second. Japanese aircraft (bandits) were
coded by gender — masculine for the fighters (Zeke, Os-
car, Tojo) and feminine for the bombers (Betty, Jill,
Judy). At lights-out, Nick fell into bed exhausted, and
even then there was no letup. The GQ gong was apt to
sound at any hour of the night, jarring him out of his
cramped bunk.

*"General quarters! General quarters! All hands man
your battle stations!"*

There would be a confused scramble as the aircrewmen rubbed sleep from their eyes and groped for shoes
and dungarees.

"Quonset Point's beginning to seem like a rest
camp," Nick said one night at three A.M., as he clambered
up a ladder to the hangar deck. "I think I could find my
way to the ready room in the dark."

"Good," Hildy said, grinning. "One night we may
have to."

The squadron wasn't considered at GQ until everyone was in flight gear, ready for launching. Mr. Scott,
who always managed to get to the ready room first, would
be donning his gear when the others hurried in. Pilots
wore khaki flight suits and helmets with tinted goggles.
Most of the crewmen preferred dungarees to flight suits,
which were sweaty, and, instead of helmets, headsets
clamped over long-visored baseball caps. Barney Jacob's
cap, which bore a green 4-H emblem, was a bright red
one that he'd won at the Illinois State Fair. When gen-

eral quarters was set, Captain Rawlins would come on the loudspeaker system.

"Not bad, but not good enough. I want this goddamn ship ready to shoot down Japs within thirty seconds. Let's do it again."

Every morning, the first reconnaissance flight was airborne before dawn — four sections, each consisting of two bombers, either TBF Avengers or SB2C Helldivers, escorted by three F6F Hellcats ("Gumdrops," the fighters were called), searching two hundred miles out in four quadrants, north and south, east and west. The TBFs were always launched first, guided into takeoff position by plane handlers with red and green flashlights — red for port, green for starboard. The handlers moved smoothly, precisely, inches from the whirling propellers, their flashlights making neonlike streaks in the gray predawn. A live flight deck was fraught with danger; a moment's inattention, an abrupt gesture, and an arm could be lost — or worse.

"Launch aircraft!" the air officer would boom through a bullhorn from the bridge.

The planes revved up to full power before releasing their brakes. Raspberry One always looked special as it raced down the flight deck and surged into the sky, vapor trails streaming from its wings and the blue glow of its exhaust rippling over the bright red of Diane's insignia. The insignia was the envy of the other crews.

"All of our planes should have it," said Luis Tomaino, the gunner on Raspberry Thirteen, Ensign Zito's plane. A small, dark boy from the South Side of Chicago, he was one of Nick and Hildy's best friends in the squadron. "Can't we have copies made?"

"No copies," Hildy replied firmly. "It's an original."

Hildy had affixed the insignia to the hatch of the radio compartment, which was on the starboard side of Raspberry One, aft of the wing. Both the radioman and the gunner entered the plane through the narrow hatch, Nick boosting Hildy up into the electric ball turret, which fired a .50-caliber gun. Once airborne, the crewmen were effectively shut off from each other — Mr. Scott sealed off in the cockpit, Hildy scrunched up like a pretzel in the turret, Nick in the radio compartment, with racks of radio and radar equipment and a .30-caliber tail gun, called a "stinger," which fired through a small Plexiglas bubble. The reconnaissance flights were long and tedious, with Hildy scanning the sky in the turret, and Nick monitoring the radar scope for blips from the ocean's surface. To break the montony, Mr. Scott sometimes let Nick tune in the powerful Armed Forces Radio Service (AFRS) station in Hawaii. The music gave him a curious feeling of unreality — moving steadily toward a major combat zone in history's greatest war, sweeping the blue Pacific sky in a torpedo bomber armed with depth charges, rockets, and machine guns, while tapping his foot to the smooth rhythms of Tommy Dorsey or Duke Ellington.

HILDY: This is really living, huh, Nick?
NICK: And how. If Diane were here, you could jitterbug on the wing.
MR. SCOTT: Wait till we're able to pick up Tokyo Rose. She's got the best collection of records west of San Francisco.

The music was turned off during the training exercises that concluded each flight, another of Captain

Rawlins's notions about value — two missions for the price of one. The various sections would rendezvous over Mother Goose and peel off in strafing runs on smoke-bomb targets; or simulated bombing runs on target sleds towed by the DDs, the destroyers; or torpedo runs on the cruisers. It was doubtful that the squadron would be making any actual torpedo attacks. The Imperial Japanese Fleet, on the defensive since Midway, had suffered disastrous losses in the Philippines. Several capital ships — the battleship *Yamato* and the carrier *Amagi* among them — had eluded pursuing American forces; but the days of great naval engagements seemed over. Captain Rawlins, however, demanded perfection.

"The Nips've still got plenty of transports and tankers," he said. "Sinking an armament ship is as good as wiping out a whole battalion."

Nick had experienced nothing as thrilling as a carrier landing. He never tired of it, Raspberry One coming in low over the water and banking into the final approach, the "groove," with the landing signals officer guiding them with his luminous orange paddles — too high, too low; too fast, too slow; then *CUT!*, the signal to come aboard. There was always a breathless moment when Mr. Scott cut the throttle and the plane settled to the deck. Then a sudden and violent thrust forward as the tail hook caught one of the eight arresting wires that stretched across the deck like great rubber bands. Hildy, in the turret, faced aft during landings.

"What a sensation!" he exclaimed after Raspberry One touched down on the *Shiloh* for the first time. "It felt like my stomach was turning inside out."

On the way back to the ready room, still in their flight gear, they frequently paused in the starboard boatswain's gallery to watch the rest of the planes land, their chins propped on the drain scupper that ran along the edge of the flight deck and their eyes wide, like kids gaping at the Brooklyn Dodgers through knotholes at Ebbetts Field. When aircraft were being recovered, the flight deck functioned like a ballet company — Hellcats and Avengers coming up the groove seconds apart; arrester crews racing out to disengage tail hooks; other crews pushing wings into the fold position; the barrier dropping to allow planes to taxi forward to the huge Number 2 elevator, which would lower them to the hangar deck for maintenance. The various crews wore jerseys of identifying colors — red for gasoline crews, yellow for plane handlers, blue for ordnancemen. It was an exciting scene, and Nick felt proud that he was a small but important part of it.

"She's one hell of a ship, isn't she?" Hildy said.

She was indeed one hell of a ship — one of the last of the Navy's great prewar carriers, a fully equipped aviation facility that could steam through the roughest seas at a speed of thirty-four knots. A floating city, with a displacement of thirty-seven thousand tons, a ship's company of three thousand officers and men, and all the services necessary to maintain them — hospital, bakery, laundry, tailor, air conditioning, four turbine engines that delivered 150,000 horsepower, huge evaporators that removed the salt from sea water and made it fresh. The fleet had many fine aircraft carriers, but the *Shiloh* was special, a tradition. Her planes and guns had inflicted more damage on the enemy than any other ship. She had taken a terrible beating in the Marianas, but had stayed afloat to fight another day. She was a great ship, and Nick and Hildy came to love her, the way they loved their home towns, the way they loved Raspberry One.

Normally, a carrier's regular ship's company developed a standoffish attitude toward an air group, regarding the pilots and aircrewmen as transients, guests in the house. VT-43, though, enjoyed excellent relations with the *Shiloh* crew, mainly because of Hildy, who roamed every inch of the ship, curiously, helpfully, finding out how things worked, lending a hand whenever he could, and making friends in the process — in the antiaircraft gun galleries that ringed the flight deck, both 20 and 40 millimeter; in the combat information center (CIC), which directed all of the *Shiloh*'s combat operations, including air strikes; in Air Plot, the ship's equivalent of an airport control tower.

"Did you meet the Air Plot guy we hear on the radio?" Nick asked him.

"He wasn't on duty," Hildy said, "but I found out all about him. Goldberg. A lieutenant. His dad owns a wholesale plumbing business in Los Angeles."

"Was he an actor or something? He's got a really smooth voice."

"A physics teacher," Hildy said. "At a high school in Pasadena."

Hildy had developed an astonishing accuracy with his turret gun, blasting smoke bombs out of the water in one short burst, almost casually. Between flights, he liked to hang out in the gun galleries, which were below the catwalk that ran around the flight deck. One day, when the gun crews were practicing on a long target sleeve towed by an F6F, the gunnery officer invited Hildy to try his luck.

"Aim at the sleeve," he joked, "not the plane."

Hildy found it difficult to maneuver the big 40-millimeter gun mount, on which the operator sat in a steel "farm-tractor" seat. But the 20s, which were sighted and fired from large handlebars, were more flexible. He opened up with great glee, the gun making a deafening noise and the spent casings clanking to the deck of the gallery, which was shaped like a tub. In two bursts, he had the range; in the third one, he shot down the sleeve, cable and all — and his fame spread throughout the ship. That night, in the Three Deck mess compartment, he was a major topic of conversation.

"Did you hear about that blond aircrewman who shot down the target sleeve?" a shipfitter asked Nick in the chow line.

"Yeah," Nick replied, feeling a surge of pride. "He's my gunner."

Hildy's feat boosted the morale of the other aircrewmen and made them feel easier about the combat missions that lay ahead.

"With him in the lead plane," Tomaino remarked, "we'll blast the Japs out of the sky."

Life aboard a large ship tended to break down into little neighborhoods and circles of close friends within those neighborhoods. For the most part, Nick and Hildy's neighborhood was limited to the flight deck, the aircrewmen's sleeping compartment in Four Deck, the hangar deck, where they spent long hours fussing over Raspberry One when the plane was down for maintenance, and the ready room. Particularly the ready room, which was the headquarters of VT-43, the squadron's battle station. A place where the crews were briefed and received orders from CIC over a teletype printer whose terse messages were projected onto a large screen for all to read. It was also a place to relax and write letters, to sip coffee and play acey-deucy, or, on the few occasions that foul weather interfered with flight operations, poker — marathon games that lasted till lights-out. At those times, the ready room took on a warm, clubhouse atmosphere, which most of the aircrewmen preferred to the movies that were shown every evening in the hangar deck.

"There's plenty of time to see those flicks," Charlie Wilson said. "They'll probably run them a hundred times before we get new ones."

Charlie, a farm boy from central Iowa, was one of Nick and Hildy's circle of close friends, which, in addition to Tomaino and Barney Jacob, included Dick O'Neal, a handsome, muscular boy from Grants Pass, Oregon. An avid fisherman, O'Neal subscribed to six outdoors magazines and talked of little but fly casting. He was an incorrigible prankster, fond of sneaking up on an unwary aircrewman and yanking the cord that inflated his Mae West life jacket.

"Who's the little man on your lap?" he would say.

Charlie Wilson's avocation was beer. He was a connoisseur, knowledgeable about malt, yeast, and hops.

"The Milwaukee beers are overrated," he once advised O'Neal. "The small town breweries are best — Waukesha, Baraboo, Oshkosh."

"How come you know so much about Wisconsin," O'Neal asked him, "when you come from Iowa?"

"I went to boot camp at Great Lakes," Charlie said. "We used to go up to Milwaukee on liberty."

Tomaino was the youngest member of the squadron; he had enlisted on his seventeenth birthday, before graduating from high school. Until recently, he'd given little thought to finishing school; boys of his background seldom went on to college. His family had seen bitter times during the Depression. His father, now a furnace stoker in a foundry, had gone five years without steady work while his mother kept the family going by taking in washing and selling corsets door to door. The situation was still bleak, but the GI Bill offered a bright ray of hope. The day after it was enacted, Tomaino had signed up for correspondence studies with the Armed Forces Institute, a government-sponsored organization that offered both college and high school courses for servicemen. He dreamed of the look of pride on his father's face when he would casually announce, "Dad, I've been accepted at Loyola" — but first he needed a diploma. One night, in the ready room, his arms loaded with books, he approached Nick.

"I've been having trouble with some of my assignments, Nick," he said. "You went to that fancy school out east. I figured maybe you'd give me a hand."

"It wasn't a fancy school," Nick said, "but it was a good one. Sure, I'd be glad to help you, Tomaino."

Nick found that he derived great satisfaction from tutoring Tomaino, that he possessed a knack for making complicated things seem simple. It was the same with the squadron's radio gear. When the other radiomen had problems with transmitters or oscillators or receivers, they turned to Nick. The gunners automatically went to Hildy, who worked with them, encouraged them, showed them how to gauge the range of a target and the correct lead — or lag — in a fraction of a second.

"Fire a short burst first," he told them. "The tracers will tell you how close you're coming. Then make a quick adjustment and really open up."

He drew diagrams on the ready room blackboard, like a football coach mapping a play, illustrating the five distinct maneuvers in a fighter attack — overtake, turn in, roll through, gun's bearing, break away.

"He's dangerous only when he's in gun's bearing," Hildy emphasized. "That's when you really want to pot him. But don't hold the trigger down too long. You'll burn out the barrel."

"What if your gun keeps jamming?" asked O'Neal, who was turret gunner on Raspberry Fifteen, Ensign Consiglio's plane. "Mine jammed three times yesterday."

"Check the head space on the bolt," Hildy advised him. "It's probably too tight."

When the *Shiloh* was within flying range of Hawaii, there was a major and unexpected change in the composition of Air Group 43. VB-43, the bombing squadron, which consisted of sixteen SB2Cs, was detached and flown to Ford Island, the Naval air facility on Oahu. The dive bombers were replaced by the addition of an equal number of F6Fs to the fighter squadron. But these were different Hellcats, designed as fighter-bombers and equipped with radar for night flying.

"What's up, Skipper?" Hildy asked Mr. Scott.

"Another invasion," he replied. "They haven't told us the target yet. The Bonins or the Ryukyus, probably. The dive bombers are most effective against ships; the fighters do a better job in support of ground troops."

"What about us?" Nick said.

"That's the remarkable thing about a TBF, Nick. It's good for any kind of mission. The British are even using a few in air-sea rescue. They load the bomb bay with rafts instead of bombs."

By late January, the *Shiloh* was steaming the northern latitudes. The nights were cool, the days frequently overcast — the Pacific version of winter. Enemy submarines were now a constant threat, and Captain Rawlins buttoned down the ship in earnest. General quarters was routinely stood for an hour before dawn and an hour after dusk, the times the ship was most vulnerable to attack. Recreational gear was stowed, and calisthenics on the flight deck were discontinued. Movies were also suspended; the hangar deck was so crowded with planes, there was no room to set up benches. A watchful aura pervaded the ship. In a combat zone, Nick was learning, you never fully relaxed. In the air, he no longer tuned in AFRS; the music was distracting. And at night, in his bunk, an abrupt change in the rumbling of the turbines woke him in a sweat.

"Looks like we'll be getting down to business pretty soon," Hildy said.

"Yeah," Nick said. "I just hope we get some mail first."

"There's probably a bunch of it at Ulithi," Hildy said. "Maybe they'll bring it aboard when we take on supplies from the support group."

Although the *Shiloh*'s initial combat assignment remained classified, its immediate destination was no secret. After being replenished by the logistics support group near Ulithi, a supply island nine hundred miles east of the Philippines, the flotilla would rendezvous with the Fifth Fleet — specifically, with Task Force 58, the fast carrier force led by the famed Vice Admiral Marc A. Mitscher, which was divided into five groups. The *Shiloh* would be attached to the group commanded by Rear Admiral Andrew P. Lawton. It was believed that Mitscher's carriers were still operating in the Philippines, in support of General MacArthur's forces, but no one in the squadron knew for sure.

"You'd think those crazy Japs would surrender after MacArthur finishes with them," Tomaino said. "But they probably won't."

In the thirty months since the invasion of Guadalcanal, the first amphibious assault of the Pacific campaign, the Navy had developed its supply tactics into a fine art, particularly the practice of replenishing warships at sea. The logistics support group — a large fleet of oilers, tankers, store ships, repair ships — was capable of supplying all of the *Shiloh*'s needs, sophisticated or mundane, by hose or by transfer line, with the carrier reducing its speed by only five or ten knots. In addition to fuel oil and ammunition, gasoline and aircraft parts, there was a floating inventory of "household" items, thousands of them — blankets, uniforms, medicine, toilet paper, even thimbles. Specialized support ships were equipped to render major repairs in case the *Shiloh* sustained battle damage. Food provisions were both dry and fresh-frozen, including — occasionally — fresh milk and eggs. Normally, however, the scrambled eggs at morning chow were powdered, as was the milk — nutritious but bland.

"When Franny and I are married," Nick said one morning, making a face as he drank his milk, "we're going to keep a cow."

The *Shiloh* and her escorts were replenished in less than half a day. Lieutenant Boyd the air group's flight surgeon, watched expectantly for a consignment of medical supplies to come aboard, several large wooden crates stenciled RESTORATIVES. He put on a little production when a gang of seamen lugged the crates into the VT-43 ready room.

"Take heart, O gallant warriors!" he declaimed in stentorian tones. "I bring a touch of felicity to warm your withered souls!"

The crates contained whiskey, bourbon, and rye, hundreds of tiny bottles, each holding two ounces. They would be rationed to the flight crews after every combat mission — hence "restorative."

"I don't want anyone trying to cadge a free drink," Doc Boyd warned. "You know the rules. Them that fights imbibes; them that malingers in sick bay drinks powdered milk."

Doc, a Nebraska country doctor, was a favorite with the squadron. A kind, reassuring man, in his late thirties, he had a wife and four school-age children back in North Platte. He asked Tomaino and O'Neal to help him as he counted the bottles and locked them in a large metal cabinet. Then, with a flourish, he pulled a little cardboard sign from his black bag and taped it to the door of the cabinet: *Tables for Ladies.*

"A souvenir from the Big Horn Saloon back home," he said. "Adds a touch of class to the joint, don't you think?"

Everyone roared with laughter. Mr. Scott, who had been prepared for the arrival of the restoratives, stepped forward with a humorous presentation for Doc — a dish-towel and a white apron, both obtained from the galley in the wardroom, the officers' mess.

"We want you to be in proper uniform during saloon hours, Doc," he said, tying the apron around his waist. "Pity you don't have a handlebar mustache."

There was more laughter, and Nick, watching the horseplay, had a good feeling about the future. They had achieved an identity, a camaraderie. They were no longer callow landlubbers; they were the air arm of the *Shiloh,* ready for action. It was Mr. Scott's doing, he knew; his constant striving to instill a sense of confidence and pride in them. He was the best kind of CO, firm but not rigid, a bit aloof, like most Annapolis officers, but there wasn't a man in the squadron who didn't consider him a personal friend.

"It will be confusing in combat," he had told them repeatedly. "All you can do is concentrate on your little part of the mission and do your best. War is a lot of men with weapons trying to stay alive. The ones who make the fewest mistakes always have an edge. Not much of an edge, but it could mean your life."

Honing the edge. That's what the past seven weeks had been all about. Mr. Scott's demands, Captain Rawlins's demands, the GQ gong clanging in the night. Honing the edge. Nick hoped it was sharp. Very sharp.

Two days later, as a group of CIC specialists filed into the ready room with thick files of reconnaissance photos and sector maps, Mr. Scott announced the target.

"Iwo Jima," he said. "The Fourth and Fifth Marines will lead the assault; we'll provide air support."

"Iwo what?" Charlie Wilson asked.

"Jima," Mr. Scott said. "It means 'island' in Japanese."

That night, as Nick and Hildy strolled the flight deck, the *Shiloh* suddenly slowed and maneuvered gradually to port. To the west, far in the distance, they could see a pulsating glow spread across the horizon, like the Northern Lights, but tinged with streaks of orange. The fleet bombardment had commenced; the battleships would pound Iwo Jima for two days, then the air groups would go in. To the north, they could make out the dim outlines of other aircraft carriers and see blinker lights flashing coded messages back and forth. Behind them, the big blinker light on the *Shiloh*'s signal bridge started clattering. Nick knew the message without deciphering the code.

They had rendezvoused with Task Force 58.

8. ABSTRACTIONS

IWO JIMA SEEMED HARDLY WORTH THE TAK-
ing, a tiny volcanic island, in the Bonin chain, that resembled a lopsided pork chop, four and a half miles long,
two and a half miles wide — a speck on the big pull-down
map in the ready room.

"It doesn't look like much," Mr. Scott admitted, "but
it has the right location and the right topography."

The location was six hundred and sixty miles south
of Tokyo, a toehold in the network of island outposts
that guarded the southern approaches to the Japanese
Homeland Islands. The topography was terrain suitable
for the construction of airfields; the Japanese had already
built two and were working on a third. Air facilities were
the Navy's first priority in extending its supply lines. The
fleet was a long way from home, four thousand miles from
Pearl Harbor, seven thousand from San Francisco. With
each move across the Pacific, it was necessary to pause and
establish adequate logistics — harbors, runways, fuel depots — like a climber hauling a supply train up a mountain, ledge by ledge. Iwo Jima was a ledge on Japan's
doorstep.

"Under normal circumstances, it wouldn't be worth
fifty cents at a sheriff's sale," Mr. Scott said on the second
day of briefings. "But war creates its own values."

"What's the word from Admiral Lawton's staff,
Skipper?" Ensign Tull asked. "Are they expecting a long
campaign?"

"To the contrary," Mr. Scott replied. "Everyone
seems to think it'll be a pushover. Personally, I'm not so
sure. Intelligence says General Kuribayashi is in command

of Iwo's defenses. I can't imagine him being a pushover. He doesn't know the meaning of defeat."

To allow pilots and crews time to concentrate on the briefings, which began after morning chow and continued until lights-out, all air group flight operations had been canceled save for the CAP. The combat air patrol was the *Shiloh*'s protective shield of F6F fighters that guarded against attack by enemy planes. Task Force 58 was steaming in hostile waters now, and kamikazes were a constant threat. Nick was amazed by the infinite detail of the invasion plans. Thousands of pages listing the disposition of the eight hundred warships and amphibious craft that would participate in the operation. The latest aerial photographs of Iwo. Gridded maps showing the location of all known batteries, pillboxes, antiaircraft installations. A comprehensive analysis of the soil of the island — a beach of coal-black lava sand, rising in terraces to a plain of dry, porous soil almost barren of vegetation. The data covered a second island in the Bonins, Chichi Jima, two hundred miles northeast of Iwo, which was also an enemy stronghold.

"We'll probably be flying a few strikes on Chichi, too," Mr. Scott said. "Its airstrips have already been bombed, but the Japs are good at repairing runways."

"Will we have to worry about hitting civilians?" asked Barney Jacob.

"Not on Iwo," Mr. Scott said. "Maybe on Chichi, but Intelligence says all civilians have been evacuated from Iwo."

D-day was February 19, a Monday. Lieutenant O'Rourke, the Catholic chaplain, said two extra Masses the day before; O'Neal and Tomaino served as altar boys at one of them. The squadron's final briefing was held

Sunday night, in the junior officers' wardroom, where the CIC staff had constructed a model of Iwo Jima, in pliable rubber, on a large mess table — a remarkably detailed relief map that showed every ridge and contour of the bleak island. Nick thought Iwo looked more like a mis-shapen pear than a pork chop. A quick glance at the rock-bound shoreline revealed only one possible place for a landing — a two-mile strip of beach at the stem of the pear, on the east side of the island. North of the beach, where the land rose in a rocky plateau, were the cliffs of an old sulfur quarry, ideal for gun emplacements. South of the beach, at the foot of the island, was a brown, squat volcanic cone, nearly six hundred feet high — Mount Suribachi, code-named Hotrocks. The slopes of the mountain were known to be studded with pillboxes. It was a tactical situation that allowed for no subtle stratagems. The invasion forces would be completely exposed, like football players on a gridiron, with the Japs firing from the bleachers. Brute force would be required to smash through to the high ground, the quarry, and Mount Suribachi, which would enfilade the beach in a deadly cross-fire.

"At times like this," Hildy remarked, "I'm glad I'm not a Marine."

Ever since the *Shiloh* sailed from Quonset Point, it had been Mr. Scott's practice to tour the flight and hangar decks before taps in order to inspect the squadron's planes and determine aircraft availability for the following day's operations. At first, Lieutenant Werra, Barney Jacob's pilot and the squadron's second-in-command, accompanied him. But when the ship neared the combat zone, Mr. Scott began reserving the time for Nick and Hildy. The nightly strolls, which ended with a friendly chat on the fantail, had drawn the Raspberry One crew closer together. On the eve of the Iwo Jima invasion, Nick tried to talk casually about what lay ahead, but his voice kept quavering.

"Has Admiral Lawton assigned targets yet, Skipper?" he asked.

"He'll wait till the last minute, Nick," Mr. Scott said. "The results of the bombardment have to be evaluated first. The targets will be on the CIC printer in the morning."

"I hope we don't draw Hotrocks," Hildy said.

"Or the quarry," Nick added.

Mr. Scott shrugged. "It really won't make much difference," he said. "Targets are all alike. A gamble. A tactical problem that you do your best to solve."

Nick was reassured by his calm attitude. "I'm sure glad we're flying with you, Skipper," he said. "You make it sound routine."

"Don't be fooled by appearances, Nick," Mr. Scott said. "Everyone goes into combat the same way. Outwardly calm, inwardly petrified. You never get over it."

"Even you?"

"Especially me. I'm the leader."

"How do you keep your stomach from churning?"

"I reread my mail," Mr. Scott said. "Mail helps you keep a sense of proportion."

It was after lights-out when Nick and Hildy returned to the aircrewmen's compartment. Hildy got into a whispered conversation with O'Neal and Charlie Wilson, speculating on the targets. Nick felt in his locker for his letters, which he kept in a ditty bag under his dress whites. He took them to the head and read them in the dim glow of a night light. All of them. Franny's first. About her plans to apply for a summer job in publishing, about grades and term papers and the prize one of Diane's paintings had won in an art competition in Providence — a scene of the Point in autumn, done in watercolors. "Her sense of detail is marvelous," Franny wrote. "As a tribute to Raspberry One, she sketched in a TBF high in the sky over Narragansett Bay." Franny's letters were informative, hopeful, endearing; his mother's were — motherly. Was he getting enough fresh milk, enough sleep, and would a few dozen brownies stay fresh if she mailed them to him? Reading them, Nick was filled with pleasant thoughts about Rittenhouse Square, his little piece of the country. He felt better about things. Still, there were gnawing doubts about how he would perform in his first combat mission, the same doubts he'd had at Quonset Point. Back in the compartment, he lay awake till after midnight, knowing that the others were awake too.

"It's the waiting that gets you," he heard Tomaino whisper to O'Neal.

"Yeah," O'Neal answered. "It's a bitch."

During the night, Task Force 58 steamed to its assigned launching position, sixty-five miles northwest of Iwo Jima. The CIC printer began clattering at 0512, as the crews were getting into their flight gear.

> VECTOR TO IWO ONE-THREE-FIVE TRUE ONE-THREE-EIGHT MAGNETIC ...LAUNCH 0600...FLEET BOMBARDMENT RECOMMENCES 0640...LIFTS FOR AIR STRIKES 0803...RESUMES 0825 ...LIFTS FOR AIR STRAFING OF BEACHES 0850...H-HOUR 0900...TARGET ASSIGNMENTS TO FOLLOW...

For the first time, the crews wore small arms, .38-caliber revolvers, with holster belts and belts of extra cartridges — except Hildy, who chose to wear only his hunting knife.

"The turret's cramped enough, without a thirty-eight jabbing me in the ribs," he said. "Besides, I don't plan on getting shot down."

Nick felt uncomfortable, wearing a gun.

"I feel like James Cagney sticking up a bank," he said.

He slung the two belts over his shoulders, criss-crossed, with the revolver resting under his left arm. Doc Boyd, who had stopped by the ready room to wish the squadron luck, helped him adjust his parachute harness so that the belts wouldn't bind.

"I'll be at my regular spot at the barrier when you land, Nick," he said. "I trust there'll be no need for my black bag."

"Just make sure you open the saloon on time," Nick said, smiling.

The printer started clattering.

TARGET ASSIGNMENTS VT-43 ... FIRST AND SECOND STRIKES, HOTROCKS ... THIRD AND FOURTH STRIKES, TA-166-C-D ... PLUS TARGETS OF OPPORTUN-ITY ... GUMDROPS WILL COVER ... NO SIGNIFICANT ENEMY AIR ACTIVITY ANTICIPATED ...

"What do they mean by 'significant'?" Charlie Wilson said.

"More than a thousand Zekes," O'Neal cracked.

"What was the last target?" Tomaino asked Nick.

Nick consulted his flight chart. "The quarry," he said.

"Swell," Tomaino said, grimacing. "Hotrocks and the quarry. A lot of good our peashooters'll do if we get forced down in one of those hornets' nests."

In the rush of last-minute preparations, Nick forgot to be scared — almost. Mr. Scott, at the blackboard, gave a final review of the attack plan.

"When we strafe the beaches," he said, "hit anything that moves, anything that glitters. The Japs are artists at camouflage. The Marines will be less than a mile offshore by then. We want to give them all the help we can."

Only planes from the *Shiloh* and the *Essex* would be hitting Iwo at H-hour, he said. The other air groups would be protecting the invasion armada, and two would be making a sweep of the Chichi Jima airstrips. VT-43 would carry hundred-pound bombs on the first and second strikes, Tiny Tim rockets on the third. On the fourth strike, they would drop the new gasoline-jelly bombs, napalm, to burn away the camouflage and suck the oxygen out of underground emplacements.

"The radiomen will be equipped with aerial cameras," Mr. Scott said. "CIC wants photographs to assess the effectiveness of the jelly."

The printer was clattering again.

. . . PILOTS AND CREWS MAN YOUR PLANES . . .

"Okay, let's do some flying," Mr. Scott said. "Remember to fire test bursts as soon as we're in formation. We want every gun ready for action."

"Oh, God," Barney Jacob said, pulling on his red baseball cap. "Someone please tell me this is all a dream."

The launch, at forty minutes before sunrise, was routine. It was cold on the flight deck, but the skies were clear, and Meteorology had forecast a warming trend. As Raspberry One lifted off, Nick had his first view of Task Force 58, eighty warships stretching as far as he could see — fast carriers, battleships, cruisers, destroyers. The thirteen TBFs — three were down for maintenance — joined up at eight thousand feet, with their Gumdrop escorts, forty-four Hellcats, sweeping the sky five thousand feet above them. Nick quickly picked up Iwo Jima and the invasion armada on the radar and gave Mr. Scott a vector.

NICK: Steer three degrees starboard, Skipper. That'll put us right on our holding area southeast of Hotrocks.

The plane was filled with the acrid odor of cordite as he and Hildy fired test bursts. The first time Nick had fired a gun in a TBF, the smell of cordite made him ill. But now he found the plane's special smells reassuring — cordite and hydraulic fluid and the hot odors the radio and radar equipment gave off.

HILDY: Turret gun okay, sir.
NICK: Stinger gun okay, sir.
MR. SCOTT: Roger. Wing guns are okay. I guess we're in business.

Hildy's gun, in the dorsal electric turret, was Raspberry One's main fire power, with a wide firing arc — from two to ten on the face of a clock. The arc of Nick's tail gun, which was manually operated, was very limited — from five to seven o'clock, below the plane only. The gun could not be elevated, but it was effective against ground targets.

HILDY: Here comes the sun. Wow! Like a rainbow.

Nick took a moment from the radar to glance out the small port window of the radio compartment. The sun was a fiery orange ball that for a moment spilled a blinding, prismatic light over half the ocean — brilliant reds and yellows and golds. Watching it, he was struck, as he had been many times in the past, by the great beauty of flying. In the air, he always felt a peace, a serenity, a sense of oneness with the universe. The things of Earth seemed petty and insignificant. Even the war and its vast devastation seemed of little consequence, a smudge in the scheme of things, a ripple in the —

HILDY: Bogeys at nine o'clock low, Skipper. Coming in out of the sun.
MR. SCOTT: Are they bandits, Hildy?
HILDY: Yes, sir. Zekes, I think. Twenty or twenty-five of them.

Nick felt his heart thumping. The Zekes were probably from Chichi Jima; every aircraft on Iwo had been demolished in the bombardment, but the Japs could have patched up the runways on Chichi.

MR. SCOTT: (radio) Hello, Gumdrop Leader. This is Raspberry One. Bandits. Nine o'clock low.

GUMDROP LEADER: (radio) Roger, Raspberry One. We've spotted them. A reception committee is on the way down.

MR. SCOTT: (radio) Raspberry One to Raspberry Group. Tighten up the formation. We've got visitors.

In the glare of the sun, Nick couldn't make out the bandits, but he could see the Hellcats diving down from above.

HILDY: Look at that one Gumdrop, will you! He blew the lead Zeke to smithereens!

MR. SCOTT: A couple of them are breaking through. Be alert.

Nick quickly checked their course on the radar, then got down on his hands and knees and hunched over the .30-caliber stinger gun, frightened and confused. An air battle was raging around him, but he couldn't see it; the radio compartment offered a limited range of vision. Then the plane started vibrating as Hildy opened up with the turret gun — a short burst, followed by several longer ones. The pretending was over, Nick thought; they were in combat.

MR. SCOTT: Splash one Zeke! Good shooting, Hildy.

HILDY: I think O'Neal got the other one.

MR. SCOTT: Here come two more.

HILDY: I see them, Skipper. The first one's chickening out. He's breaking off below us, Nick. You'll have a clear shot with the stinger. Pot him!

Nick could see the bandit coming into range at five o'clock low, with the bright red Rising Sun emblem of the Japanese Empire glittering from its wings and fuselage. A Zeke, the famed Mitsubishi Zero that he'd read about as an adolescent, that had wrought so much damage at Pearl Harbor on the day that would live in infamy. A Zeke, squarely in his gun sight, so close he could see that the pilot was wearing a white scarf. A perfect shot. But he didn't press the trigger, couldn't press it. He hunched over the gun, paralyzed with fear — trembling, perspiring, feeling his pants fill but unable to control it, staring dumbly through the stinger bubble as the Zeke went into a diving roll and got away —

MR. SCOTT: What's wrong, Nick? Your gun jam up?

Nick remained frozen, his hands rigidly gripping the gun, unable to think, unable to reach for his microphone.

MR. SCOTT: Are you okay, Nick?"

Then he felt a hand on his shoulder. Hildy had slipped down from the turret, his headset off, his face sweaty. Nick expected him to slap him; that's what they did in the movies when a guy panicked. But Hildy just grinned.

"There's nothing to it, Nick," he said above the noise of the engine. "It's just like Quonset Point, only with live ammo."

Nick turned and looked up at Hildy, his smiling face, his clear blue eyes, and stopped trembling. It was as though his friend were a talisman, a good luck charm. Nothing would go wrong with Hildy in the plane. He burst into embarrassed laughter, at the absurdity of the situation, at the indignity of his personal untidiness. Filling his pants before they even reached the target. Mr. Scott probably knew what had happened; odors traveled quickly in a TBF. The whole squadron would know. He'd have a reputation as Chicken Little.

> MR. SCOTT: That's the last of them. The Gumdrops have chased off the rest. Is your personal crisis resolved, Nick?
> NICK: Yes, sir.
> MR. SCOTT: Good. When we get back to Mother Goose, hustle down to the aircrewmen's compartment for a change of skivvies. I'll cover for you in the ready room.
> NICK: Thanks, sir.

The attack by the Zekes had a bracing effect on the squadron. They had been put to the test, unexpectedly, and were equal to the challenge — two Zekes shot down, two others badly damaged. With their baptism of fire behind them, they went into the first Iwo Jima strike less jittery, more confident, not as greenhorns, but as combat veterans — bombing Hotrocks with a precision that produced twenty-three confirmed hits on enemy emplacements, strafing the beaches with a withering barrage that kicked up great clouds of black lava sand. The biggest cloud of all came from the explosion of a pillbox that Nick hit. He could see gun barrels and human limbs flying through the air. A lucky shot, he knew, that had probably detonated a stockpile of ammo. Still, it helped to compensate for his indecorous performance during the air attack.

> MR. SCOTT: (radio) Raspberry One to Raspberry Group. Here come the Marines. Let's get out of their way.

The TBFs climbed to five thousand feet and vectored for Mother Goose, to refuel and rearm for the second strike; relief squadrons from other carriers were already in position to provide continued air support to the invasion. For a few minutes, Nick had a panoramic view of the spectacle — the landing craft racing for the beach, the green blur of Marines swarming like ants over the black sand, the blinding salvoes from rocket ships flashing across the sky. What a rotten job, he thought; he and Hildy would be having coffee and sandwiches in the ready room while the Marines were fighting through to Hotrocks and the quarry. As the invasion forces stormed the beach, the fleet bombardment resumed, targeted two hundred yards inland, in a rolling barrage intended to conform to the actual advance of the troops. But the Marines weren't advancing. The first assault wave was still on the beach, pinned down in a hail of mortar and artillery fire from the high ground.

> HILDY: Why aren't they moving? They'll get slaughtered in that crossfire.

Hundreds of them already had been, the aircrewmen learned when the squadron got back to the ship. The Marines had encountered an unexpected problem — the beach itself, volcanic ash so deep that it allowed little traction; it was like wading in sawdust. Running was impossible; the troops could barely walk. Even tanks and other tracked vehicles were immobilized; steel matting was being rushed ashore to provide traction over the ash to solid ground.

"Some pushover," Tomaino remarked.

With a slender beachhead finally established, the Marines pushed inland, only to encounter far more serious difficulties. Most of the Japanese garrison, they soon discovered, was holed up in an intricate network of caves and tunnels that stretched the length of the island. Mount Suribachi alone was a labyrinth of gun emplacements, a thousand or more, all connected to living quarters deep in the mountain, where the defenders had sat out the bombardments, sipping tea and cooking rice. General Kuribayashi had played a waiting game; now his troops opened up from positions so cleverly concealed, they couldn't be detected until it was too late. Marines died violently, grotesquely, cut to ribbons by mortar fire, small arms, machine guns. By 1300 hours, in the hot midday sun, a thick stench of death rose from the island. An urgent call went out for pinpoint air support, preferably TBFs.

"We'll be working with the regimental commanders," Mr. Scott said on D-day plus one, when VT-43 was assigned to the Marine fire control unit. "They'll spot the targets; we'll knock them out."

Thus began the long, grueling series of missions in which the Raspberry One crew developed an uncanny precision in their grim work: Mr. Scott invariably planting a bomb squarely on a cave entrance or a pillbox; Hildy blasting away at the bandits that frequently jumped the squadron on the approaches to the island; Nick effectively strafing ditches, foliage, rubble —any cover that might conceal enemy soldiers. It was dirty, sweaty work, from dawn till dusk, day after day, with Nick frequently nauseated by the sickening stench of Iwo that filled the plane at lower altitudes. At night, both he and Hildy would take scalding showers to rid themselves of the odor, then crawl into their bunks, numb with exhaustion.

"Look at it this way," Hildy said one night with his usual optimism. "At least we get to sleep in a bunk, instead of a grubby foxhole on Iwo. Those poor Marines. Just going to the toilet must be a problem for them."

But even in their bunks, there was no letup from the tension. Flight operations continued around the clock, with the air group's new night fighters flying CAP to guard against suicide planes. The Japanese had stepped up their kamikaze activity. On D-day plus three, the *Bismarck Sea* was sunk and the *Saratoga* crippled in a night kamikaze attack. Nick felt safe only in the ready room, which by now reflected a strong squadron identity — funny cartoons pinned to the bulletin board, school pennants taped to the bulkhead, prank messages scrawled on the blackboard. *O'Neal — call your bookie.* Next to the aircraft AVAILABILITY board, Mr. Scott had installed a SPLASH! board, which kept a running tally of bandits shot down by the gunners. Predictably, Hildy's name led the list, with an ultimate total of eleven Zekes. O'Neal was second, with four Zekes and two Tojos. Of Nick and Hildy's circle of friends, only Tomaino's name was missing.

"I've just got to splash a Zeke," he said, growing desperate. "How's my old man going to brag about me at the VFW?"

"He should be glad you're still alive," Barney Jacob said. "Better no splash than no Tomaino."

Nick shared Barney's feelings. He was amazed they'd flown so many missions with no casualties, no planes shot down, not even a flight deck accident. They all knew their luck could run out at any moment, but no one spoke of it openly. As they waited for the order from CIC to man planes, their chatter was always light, breezy, humorous — but their nervous habits gave them away. Hildy usually hummed a Glenn Miller tune, O'Neal told fish stories, and Barney, who had appointed himself chief assistant to Doc Boyd, invariably chose that moment to inventory the first-aid cabinet.

"Better make out a requisition, Barney," O'Neal would rib him. "We're down to our last gallon of Mercurochrome."

After a mission, the atmosphere of the ready room was boisterous, exhilarating, like a football locker room after the big game, with the excited crews — except Hildy — clamoring for their restoratives, and Doc Boyd, in his white apron, agreeably playing the role of bartender, but keeping an eagle eye on them for signs of strain or fatigue, signs of an impending crackup.

At the end of the second week of support missions, Captain Rawlins came by the ready room and threw a little party.

"Admiral Lawton has just radioed statistics of the Iwo operation to date," he said. "And y'all will be pleased to learn that you Raspberries have topped every torpedo squadron in the Task Force."

A yell of jubilation went up.

"And so as a gesture of appreciation for a job well done, I'm authorizing Doc Boyd to issue an extra restorative."

There was an even louder yell.

"For purely medicinal purposes," he added quickly, grinning.

The statistics were posted on the bulletin board. Nick studied them carefully. The *Enterprise* and the *Yorktown* were VT-43's closest competitors, but the Raspberries had topped them in every category — number of sorties flown, percentage of aircraft availability, number of confirmed hits, enemy planes splashed.

"Well, Nick," Mr. Scott said, peering over his shoulder, "seems we're doing a proper job of things."

"Yes, sir," Nick replied, smiling proudly. "And with proper skivvies."

The following day, VT-43 was pulled off support duty for a series of strikes against Chichi Jima. Mr. Scott, anticipating stiff enemy air opposition, prodded Maintenance for 100 percent aircraft availability — and got it. However, the additional firepower wasn't necessary. After Iwo, Chichi Jima was a milk run — glide bombing runs from nine thousand feet, followed by low-level strafing, with little antiaircraft fire and no Zekes to harass them. The Raspberries had a field day, but after the last strike, Hildy was visibly disturbed.

"I splattered some civilians," he told Nick when they paused to chat in the boatswain's gallery. "Woman and children. I thought they were Jap soldiers."

"Maybe you just wounded them," Nick said.

"No, Nick. I splattered them real good. I could see brains flying around."

That day, Hildy drank his first restorative and smoked his first cigarette. Within a week, he was smoking a pack a day. Nick knew what he was going through. Until Chichi Jima, the consequences of their missions, of their bombs and bullets, had been abstractions. Seen from

the air, there was a certain toylike quality to war. But
now —

As the squadron resumed support duty, a great weariness came over Nick. Iwo Jima was deadening his senses
— the stench, the slaughter, the constant fear of kamikazes. It was as though the war always had been and always would be. There was no Franny, no Rittenhouse
Square — only the war. After Iwo, there would be another island — and another and another, and then Japan
itself. By the time the killing was over, he and Hildy
would be old men. Or dead.

9. OLD HOME WEEK

THE CONQUEST OF IWO JIMA WAS EXPECTED
to take four days. It took nearly a month, and isolated
pockets of resistance held out for weeks afterward. It was
the most savage and costly battle in the history of the U.S.
Marine Corps. The Marine dead numbered six thousand;
the wounded, seventeen thousand. Navy casualties were
one thousand dead and two thousand wounded. The Japanese garrison of twenty-two thousand troops was virtually exterminated. General Kuribayashi, faced with defeat, had committed hara-kiri.

The island was declared secured on March 16. A
week before that, however, Task Force 58 withdrew to
Ulithi. Air bombardment was proving useless in blasting
out the remaining defenders, who were holed up in caves
and tunnels thirty feet underground. The mop-up was
left to Marine units with flame throwers and heavy explo-

sives, who entombed the enemy by sealing shut the entrances to the caves.

"Further air support would be a waste of bombs," Mr. Scott explained when he briefed the squadron on the situation. "So we're going to get a couple of days' relaxation at Ulithi before our next operation."

There was scuttlebutt that the next target would be an island in the Ryukyus, probably Okinawa, and that the invasion would be preceded by a carrier strike on the Japanese homeland. Nick and Hildy ignored the rumors. Combat, they had learned, was best taken a day at a time. In the three weeks the *Shiloh* had operated off Iwo, Raspberry One had flown sixty-eight support missions, plus four strikes on Chichi Jima. They were worn out.

"We should've been boatswain's mates," Hildy said wearily. "I could sleep a week."

As the *Shiloh* retired to the south, a holiday mood filled the ship. Movies were resumed, and recreational gear was broken out. Ping-Pong tables were set up in the hangar deck, and a volleyball tournament was held on the flight deck. The weather was warm and clear. In the afternoons, Nick and Hildy sunned themselves in one of the gun galleries, at the invitation of Hildy's friends among the gunners. Hildy's Princeton application form had arrived in the last mail. Nick offered to help him fill it out.

"I've got to get a letter from my high school principal first," Hildy said. "They want references."

In the evenings, Nick continued his tutoring of Tomaino, who was about ready for his final exams.

"It's been swell of you, Nick, helping me this way," he said. "Will my old man be floored when I get accepted at Loyola!"

Barney Jacob was also thinking ahead to college — pharmacy. He pestered Doc Boyd for books on the subject, which he pored over in a secluded spot on the fantail.

"I used to jerk sodas at a drug store back home," he said. "Garton's — where Loretta works. Anyway, Mr. Garton always said that if I studied pharmacy, he'd give me a job and a chance to buy him out when he retires."

O'Neal spent the lull catching up on his outdoors magazines. At Ulithi, there would be shore leave at the fleet recreation center, and he was determined to do some fishing, somehow. There should be plenty of parrot fish and groupers near the shore, he figured. He might even hook a grunt, which, despite its name, was a beautiful fish.

"What would you do with them?" Charlie asked him.

"Get one of the cooks to fry 'em up," he said. "Hey, that'd be a battle breakfast. Fish fresh from the ocean, dusted in flour and fried in butter."

Charlie Wilson, meantime, talked of nothing but beer and ways to smuggle a supply aboard ship.

"You'd be court-martialed for sure," O'Neal said.

"Not with a little help," Charlie said. "If you guys would each slip a couple of bottles under your jumpers, we could pull it off."

In the long push across the Pacific, from Pearl Harbor to Iwo Jima, American strategy had been one of "island-hopping" — seizing Japanese-held islands of major importance while neutralizing others. The strategic value of Ulithi, a scattering of islands that had once produced coconuts and sugar cane, lay in its blue lagoon, which was wide and deep and sheltered by a coral atoll that formed a natural breakwater. Large as it was, how-

ever, when the ships of Task Force 58 dropped anchor
(on March 12, a Monday), the lagoon was so crowded,
there was a traffic problem. Ships stretched as far as the
eye could see, hundreds of them, warships, support ships,
hospital ships, ships that carried smaller amphibious craft
— even a fifty-vessel flotilla that flew the British ensign.
Tomaino looked out from the ready room, awed.

"Makes the Spanish Armada look like a bunch of
skiffs," he said with a low whistle.

"If all those babies are for Okinawa," Charlie Wilson
commented, peering over Tomaino's shoulder, "it's going
to be one hell of a show."

Shore facilities were even more crowded than the
lagoon. O'Neal had envisioned a picturesque island of
tropical beauty, with native villages and brown-skinned
girls in grass skirts. Instead, there was only the congested
panorama of a sprawling supply depot, a vast staging area
for the men and matériel of war.

"How am I going to fish in this mess?" he griped.

But he managed, borrowing a rod and reel and a few
lures from a yeoman in the atoll commander's office.

"Hey, I don't want to get my watch wet," he said,
slipping it off and handing it to Tomaino. "Give me a
holler before the last launch leaves for the ship."

He wandered off to find a strip of atoll that wasn't
cluttered with cranes or docks.

"He's nuts," Tomaino said, shaking his head. "It'll
be dark in an hour. How's he going to fish in the dark?"

In order to allow all hands time ashore, Captain
Rawlins had divided the crew into four sections and
scheduled staggered liberty periods. VT-43 drew the last
one, from six to midnight on Tuesday. Only Barney
Jacob elected to remain aboard ship.

"I'll have the ready room all to myself," he said. "I can get a lot of letters written. Besides, I'd just as soon concentrate on the business at hand."

Ulithi was swarming with sailors in shore-going whites. They jammed the enlisted men's beer pavilion and the big Ship's Service lounge, where there were magazines and a jukebox and tables with stacks of V-mail forms for writing letters.

"It ain't exactly Pago Pago," Tomaino said, disappointed. "But it beats Hotrocks and the quarry."

From the mimeographed base newspaper, *Broadside*, Nick learned of the presence of several notables on the island, including one of President Roosevelt's sons, who was an officer on the CINCPAC staff. But the big attractions were a Notre Dame all-American quarterback, who was CO of a minesweeper, and a former heavyweight boxing champion — Commander Gene Tunney, who had defeated Jack Dempsey years back and was now in charge of fleet recreation. There was also a contingent of famous war correspondents, including Ernie Pyle and the novelist John P. Marquand, one of Franny's favorites. Nick hoped to catch a glimpse of him so that he could write her about it, but didn't. However, they all got a thrill when Gene Tunney came through the beer pavilion, pausing to give autographs, shadow-boxing with a corpsman off the *Samaritan*, a hospital ship.

"He sure looks great," said Hildy, who had managed to get an autograph. "How old would he be, anyway?"

"Fifty, at least," Nick said. "He beat Dempsey way back in 'twenty-six."

"You think he could whip Joe Louis?" Tomaino asked. "I mean, if he was younger."

"Nobody could whip Joe Louis," Charlie said. "But

Tunney runs a good beer joint. Hey, Tomaino. Get us another round. Three for me."

"Skip me, Tomaino," Hildy said. "Being ashore is all the restorative I need."

Charlie appeared to be settling down for some serious drinking. Hildy had heard that an orchestra was playing at a dance at the officers' club, musicians from the Seabees, the legendary Naval Construction Battalion, which built roads and runways with combat raging around it.

"A dance?" Nick said, puzzled. "Who're they going to dance with? Each other?"

"Nurses, dummy," Hildy said. "A bunch of them came ashore from those hospital ships. Navy nurses, mostly, but a few from the Army, too."

"You don't think they're going to let us in, do you? A couple of swabbies?"

"Heck, no," Hildy said. "But maybe we can find a spot outside where we can listen to the music."

As they pushed through the noisy pavilion, Nick ran into a boy he'd known at St. Crispin's, as well as several old shipmates he and Hildy had trained with at Fort Lauderdale, who were now with air groups on the *Bennington* and the *Wasp*. It gave him a good feeling to see so many familiar faces, and he was tempted to stay at the pavilion and make a night of it. But Hildy was insistent.

"Come on, Nick," he said, pulling him toward the door. "We'd just end up heaving our guts out, like Charlie and Tomaino are going to do."

It was a cool, pleasant evening. The sun had gone down, and a bright Pacific moon was rising over the atoll. The officers' club echoed with the sounds of music and gaiety. The club was at the edge of the base administrative compound, in a series of large Quonset huts with high, arching roofs. Nick and Hildy found a place where they could watch the festivities through an open window — in a storage area to one side of the club, atop a stack of wooden crates that contained canned field rations. The orchestra was a large one, thirteen pieces, including five saxophones.

"Just like the casino, huh?" Hildy said.

"Without the Wickford local to worry about catching," Nick added.

Nick spotted Mr. Scott, in dress khakis, dancing with an Army nurse. She was a tall girl who looked quite pretty from a distance, tanned, willowy, very graceful in her movements. She had short brown hair, a dusky complexion, and was wearing Army gabardines — skirt, blouse, overseas cap with the Medical Corps insignia.

"Some dish," Hildy said — and immediately froze. "Oh swell, they're coming outside!"

Scrambling down from the crates, Nick snagged the jumper of his uniform. Behind the club stretched long rows of tanks and jeeps and amphibious tractors, ready for loading. They tried to duck behind one of the tanks, but it was too late.

"Nick! Hildy!" Mr. Scott called after them. "Wait!"

Nick felt like a little boy who'd been caught peeking.

"We were just listening to the orchestra, Mr. Scott," he said. "We didn't mean to intrude."

"Forget it, Nick. I want you to meet Miss Snyder. First Lieutenant Florence Snyder. She's from your neck of the woods, Hildy."

"No kidding?"

"Scout's honor," Miss Snyder said, and her wide smile made Nick feel good. "La Crosse, Wisconsin."

"Well, I'll be —" Hildy said, and grinned. "Holy cow, it's a regular old home week tonight."

"Where's La Crosse?" Nick asked.

"Across the river from Red Wing," Hildy said. "Hey, you wouldn't happen to know anyone from there, would you, Miss Snyder?"

"Oh, scads of people," she said, and ticked off the names. "The Johnsons on River Road, the Knudsens on High Street — I was at the university with their daughter —"

"Millie Knudsen!" Hildy exclaimed. "She lives four doors from us!"

They talked excitedly for half an hour, in the shadow of a Sherman tank — about home towns, families, schools. Miss Snyder was a surgical nurse, on the hospital ship *Comfort*. She was twenty-four, had been in the Army two years, was a veteran of the Tarawa, Saipan, and Iwo Jima campaigns, and was due for a shore assignment, Guam or Hawaii, in six weeks. She was probably a very good nurse, Nick thought. She had a way about her, a presence of mind, that inspired confidence — like Franny. Mr. Scott, who seemed more than casually interested in her, went back into the club and brought out some drinks — gin and grapefruit juice in paper cups.

"We used to sneak drinks this way at college dances," Miss Snyder said. "In the parking lot."

"I'd love to be sneaking a few in a college parking lot right now," Nick said.

"With Franny?"

"Hey, how'd you know about her?"

"Oh, I know all about you and Hildy," she said, smiling. "That Franny and Diane go to Wickford. That you're the best aircrewmen in the fleet —"

"Florence," Mr. Scott said, embarrassed. "All I said was —"

"Oh, come on, Bob," she chided affectionately. "Don't be a pill."

They were interrupted by the loudspeaker in the club. Admiral Lawton was introducing the squadron commanders.

"... But even though the hotshots of *Enterprise* and *Yorktown* have topped fourteen other carriers, they haven't quite caught up to that reserved gentleman of Raspberry One, who will soon be journeying to the land of cherry blossoms and geishas — "

Nick and Hildy turned abruptly to Mr. Scott, who avoided their eyes.

"Hey, Bob," someone called out the door. "You're on!"

Mr. Scott and Lieutenant Snyder hurried back to the club. At the door, Miss Snyder waved.

"If I get home first, I'll call your folks, Hildy," she called. "You do the same for me, okay?"

"Sure thing, Miss Snyder. We'll be seeing you."

She disappeared into the crowd. Nick and Hildy felt a letdown. They waited for the music to resume. When it didn't, Hildy glanced at his watch.

"Well," he said, "we've still got an hour. Want to go back to the pavilion?"

"I guess so," Nick said.

They started down the graveled street.

"Did you hear what Admiral Lawton said about geishas?" Hildy said.

"Yeah. I heard."

"He was probably talking about long-range plans."

"Yeah," Nick said. "Probably."

As they turned up toward the beer pavilion, Nick looked out at the atoll and saw a familiar figure silhouetted in the moonlight. It was O'Neal, barefoot and with his pants rolled up, casting a line out into the water.

"Hey, O'Neal!" he hollered, cupping his hands. "Getting about that time!"

O'Neal waved with his hat. And as he did so, a boyhood image flashed through Nick's mind. He and his father on the beach at Cape May, casting lines into the surf. Suddenly he wanted to feel close to Franny.

"I think I'll skip the pavilion, Hildy, and go over to Ship's Service. I want to write a letter."

"Suits me," Hildy said. "You know something, Nick? I don't like it out here. I feel out of place in the middle of this damn ocean. We're all out of place. I'd just as soon keep my nose to the grindstone and then get the hell home. Barney was right. Liberty is a distraction."

The Ship's Service lounge was very crowded. They had to squeeze in at one of the tables. When Nick looked up, he was surprised to see Tomaino and Charlie Wilson sitting across from them, with V-mail forms.

"I don't believe it," he said. "What's the matter, Charlie? They run out of beer?"

Charlie shrugged sheepishly. "They've got mail pick-ups here every day," he said. "It'd be a shame to waste the good service."

But Nick knew why Charlie and Tomaino were there; why all of them were there. The scuttlebutt was true. They were going to strike Japan, and they were scared.

10. PHILOSOPHERS

TASK FORCE 58 SORTIED FROM ULITHI ON
Wednesday. Two days later, at latitude 19° 50′ N, longi-
tude 137° 40′ E, the ships rendezvoused with the logistics
support group. The lagoon had been so crowded that the
task force couldn't replenish at Ulithi; it had to do so at
sea. Nick was hoping there would be some letters from
home; oilers were the primary mail carriers of the fleet.
But the mail ship from San Francisco had been delayed
in the Marshall Islands, at Eniwetok, and so he made do
with a third reading of his last batch of letters — a cheerful one from his mother, with a clipping about his father's appointment to a civic committee; and a series of
three from Franny, each written in tiny handwriting and
a single paragraph, in order to cram in as many words as
possible.

> . . . I still haven't talked to Father about us.
> He's been preoccupied with rumors that con-
> tinue to come out of Germany. No one seems to
> know exactly what's going on in those concen-
> tration camps, but there's a sense of forebod-
> ing . . .

Dr. Kaplan and his committee, she wrote, had met
with a man from the White House, a Mr. Hopkins. They
had urged swift action to liberate the camps, perhaps the
routing of our armies to Dachau or Buchenwald. Mr.
Hopkins had been sympathetic but firm. He assured them
of the President's deep personal concern, but said that

Allied strategic plans could not be altered. War wasn't that simple.

> . . . Father was very disappointed. He had expected *some*thing — a gesture, at least. All of this gives me a funny feeling. Jews have a closeness, a oneness. It's almost tribal, I suppose. One of your outposts is under siege, and you can't break through to relieve the suffering. As collateral reading for my history course, I've been wading through Adolph Hitler's literary masterpiece, *Mein Kampf*. I'm appalled. How could the good people of the world let the war happen, when that madman advertised his intentions? . . .

Crossing the Pacific, Nick had checked out two books on Judaism from the ship's library. He had found them instructive but dull. Franny's letters, however, were more valuable than books. They made him feel things about Jews.

> . . . It may interest you to know that I've been mulling over a few rules of the road conducive to domestic bliss. I won't eat meat on Friday, of course, and I trust you'll miraculously lose your taste for breaded pork chops, which should simplify our menu. As for our various Sabbaths, I'll defer to yours if you'll defer to mine. (I may even accompany you to Mass now and then; I love the smell of incense.) That way, every weekend will be one long, lovely, lazy Sabbath. As for our children (you do plan to impregnate me, don't you?), I haven't quite figured that one out

yet, but I'm hopeful. There's a rabbi at NYU I
want to talk to, at the Hillel center . . .

Reading Franny's letters, Nick was always struck by
the extent to which their worlds overlapped, despite the
vast distance that separated them.

. . . Diane and I hardly ever go out anymore, not
even to the movies. The newsreels are too de-
pressing. Last time we went, they showed films
of TBFs attacking Iwo Jima. I thought: Oh, my
God, Nick and Hildy are in one of those
planes! Afterward, back at the dorm, I was in a
trance. Whenever the phone rang, I expected it
to be you. You would ask me to meet you in the
village for hamburgers and malts, and then we
would walk in the snow to the Point. Silly of me,
I know. But you're still a very strong presence
here, darling, and I hope that a little bit of me
flies with you in Raspberry One . . .

After replenishing, the task force set course for that
area of the far western Pacific Ocean known as the East
China Sea, which was referred to simply as "China Sea"
on the CIC printer. On Saturday morning, Mr. Scott announced the target — the fifty-five airfields on Kyushu,
the southernmost of Japan's four principal islands.

"The scuttlebutt about Okinawa was correct," he
said. "The invasion is set for April first. As you know,
Okinawa is within range of enemy land-based aircraft.
CINCPAC wants the task force to destroy as many as possible so that they can't shoot up the Tenth Army boys
on the beaches."

The strikes would have a secondary purpose: photo reconnaissance, primarily to pinpoint airfields on Shikoku, Honshu, and Hokkaido.

"Just one day of strikes, Skipper?" asked Ensign Riopelle.

"Two. Sunday and Monday."

"These Sunday missions are a pain," griped O'Neal. "I'll miss Mass again."

"No, you won't," Mr. Scott said. "Father O'Rourke will say early Mass here in the ready room, at o-four-hundred."

The CIC printer clattered.

MOTHER GOOSE VECTORING TWO-ONE-SEVEN . . . WILL COMMENCE RUN-IN TO CHINA SEA 2243 . . . ESTIMATE ON-STATION 0316 . . . WILL LAUNCH FIRST STRIKE AT DAWN . . . HEAVY ENEMY COUNTERATTACKS LIKELY . . . TASK FORCE WILL HOLD BACK SUB-STANTIAL CAP FORCE . . .

"I know you're all a little edgy about hitting the enemy's homeland," Mr. Scott said. "But that's what the whole war has been leading to. Look on it as just another mission — Chichi Jima with pretty scenery. Now, let's get to work. We've got a lot of maps to study."

A list of targets came over the printer at 1700. Most of the task force's seventeen air groups were assigned to specific Kyushu airfields, but VT-43, to everyone's surprise, drew high-altitude photo reconnaissance — mainly because all of the radiomen, including Nick, had been checked out in the use of an improved aerial camera recently issued to the fleet. There would be two missions: one to photograph Japanese Naval installations in the Inland Sea, another to assess damage to the Kyushu targets.

"Can you beat that?" Tomaino said. "A regular milk run."

The squadron felt relieved in one way, disappointed in another. There was an element of adventure in the idea of attacking a storied land they knew only from travelogues and Gilbert and Sullivan. From twenty thousand feet, however, Japan would look like a relief map.

"We probably won't even get a good look at Fujiyama," Charlie Wilson complained.

"Quit your bitching, Charlie," said Barney Jacob, who evaluated every mission in terms of his wife and baby. "Twenty thousand will be a lot healthier."

But even the Kyushu raids were a milk run that day. The excitement was back at the task force. While the air groups were attacking Kyushu, the enemy, well alerted, was attacking the carriers, with both kamikaze and orthodox aircraft, confirming the wisdom of the decision to hold back a large combat air patrol. The CAP drove off the attackers, but a few kamikazes slipped through, inflicting minor damage on *Enterprise, Yorktown,* and *Intrepid.* Four Betty torpedo bombers that tried to crash the *Shiloh* were shot down by the ship's gunners.

However, the highlight of the action wasn't the kamikazes; it was the capture of the Japanese squadron commander, a major, who had been directing the attack in a Judy dive bomber. Jumped by three Hellcats, he was forced to bail out. A destroyer fished him from the water, uninjured. Later, he was transferred to the *Abilene,* Admiral Lawton's flagship, where he was interrogated, in Japanese, by a member of the admiral's Intelligence staff.

When the *Shiloh*'s planes had been recovered, Admiral Lawton made an urgent request for VT-43's reconnaissance photos of the Inland Sea. An hour later, Captain Rawlins, Mr. Scott, and Commander Seitz, the *Shiloh*'s air officer, were shuttled by launch to the *Abilene* for a top-level conference. The *Shiloh* buzzed with scuttlebutt that something big was up.

It was. When Mr. Scott returned to the ready room, he was accompanied by Captain Rawlins, Commander Seitz, and a yeoman carrying a stack of photographs and charts.

"There's been an important development," Mr. Scott said as the squadron came to attention. "I'll let Captain Rawlins tell you about it."

Captain Rawlins was wearing a foul-weather jacket over his khaki shirt; a cold, damp wind had come up in the afternoon.

"At ease, men," he said. "I'm sure y'all have heard about the Jap army officer who's in residence on the *Abilene*. Which, by itself, doesn't mean a thing. We've pulled a lot of Nip pilots from the drink in the past, and most of them were goddamn fools who heaved grenades at their rescuers. But this one's different, a real prize. Takamura is his name. Very decent chap. Disillusioned with his government's war policies. Unhappy with the way they've been wasting good young men in those kamikazes. Anyway, he's been spilling his guts. When Admiral Lawton's boys grilled him, he happened to mention the presence of the *Yamato* in the Inland Sea, at the Kure Naval base near Hiroshima. Luckily, we were in a position to check him out. We had the pictures you Raspberry radiomen snapped today — "

He motioned to the yeoman, who held up a blowup of one of the reconnaissance photos.

"There she is," Captain Rawlins said, pointing to a cluster of vessels in an anchorage off the city of Kure. "The mightiest battleship in the world."

Nick felt his pulse quicken. The *Yamato* was a legend. The pride of the Imperial Japanese Navy. Long, graceful, beautiful, with a displacement, fully laden, of 73,000 tons, nearly twice that of the *Shiloh*. A hundred antiaircraft guns, 16-inch armor plate protecting the engine rooms, a main battery of nine 18.1-inch guns that could hurl a 3200-pound shell 22.5 miles in 105 seconds. A fortress.

"Take a good look at her, boys," Captain Rawlins said. "Tomorrow morning, you're going to try to sink her."

Commander Seitz, a large man with steel-gray, crew-cut hair, outlined the plan of attack.

"The *Yamato*'s a slippery customer," he began. "She hasn't been spotted for five months, since the Battle of the Philippine Sea, where she damn near wiped out an entire fleet of our escort carriers. She's no threat in the Inland Sea, of course, but it wouldn't be difficult for the Japs to sneak a flotilla out of there and make a run for Okinawa."

He moved to the big pull-down map of the western Pacific and traced an imaginary course.

"I'd do it at night," he said. "By way of Bungo Channel, down the eastern shore of Kyushu, through Van Diemen Strait — then a flank-speed dash to Okinawa, circling away from our forces. And according to Major Takamura, that's exactly what the Japs have in mind. They know Okinawa is our next target. They plan to let the invasion get underway, then make their move. It would be catastrophic. The *Yamato* can outshoot anything we've got. She'd cause incalculable damage."

VT-43 would attack with torpedoes, he said. Against a superbattleship the size of the *Yamato,* bombs would only let in air; you needed 2000-pound torpedoes to let in water. The Raspberries had been chosen for two reasons. First, the squadron had the best record in the task force; second, the operation had to be a small, precision one. The geography of Kure ruled out a large-scale air attack. It was a sheltered anchorage, with steep terrain rising on three sides.

"There simply wouldn't be enough air space," he said. "Our planes would be tripping over each other."

Ensign Shong raised his hand.

"But will our torpedoes be effective against sixteen inches of armor?" he asked.

"You just get those fish pointed in the right direction, mister," Commander Seitz replied. "Sixteen TBFs can do one hell of a lot of damage."

"Fourteen," Mr. Scott corrected him. "Raspberry Five is down for an engine change, and Twelve got torn up in a mishap in the hangar deck."

"I'll see what I can do," Commander Seitz said. "What about your crews? Anyone on the sick list?"

"No, sir," Mr. Scott said. "We're all dangerously healthy."

"Good. Well, I guess that's it. You've got a long briefing ahead of you. I'll have Navigation plot a course. It'll be on the printer in the morning."

Nick spent three hours poring over the maps and photographs. If the weather was bad, it would be up to him to bring them over the target by radar. It had been perfect for the reconnaissance runs, but he'd noticed cirrus clouds forming in the southwest, indicating that a low-pressure system was moving in.

"I'd just as soon skip the tutoring tonight, Nick," Tomaino said. "Okay?"

"Sure thing, Tomaino," Nick replied. "First things first."

The briefing lasted past taps. They all worked quietly, efficiently. Everyone knew the odds. So far, they'd been lucky. No casualties; all of their planes still intact. War, Mr. Scott had said, was a lot of men with weapons trying to stay alive. They had heeded his advice. They had done their jobs well, and it had given them an edge. But they would pay a price for the *Yamato* — if they got her. That's what combat was all about. You paid in blood for strategic advantage. The trick was to get the most value at the cheapest price. And the unspoken question on everyone's mind was: *Will I survive the attack?*

"All right, let's knock it off," Mr. Scott said at 2230. "Our planning's as good as we can make it. With a little cooperation from the weather, we should enjoy a favorable tactical situation. But if we don't hit the sack, we'll be too groggy to see the target."

Mr. Scott had asked Nick and Hildy to stop by his stateroom before they turned in. Hildy felt honored; enlisted men were seldom invited to officers' country. It was a cramped room, painted slate-gray, with a bunk, a locker, a small desk, and a metal chair. A mess boy had brought up three mugs of coffee from the wardroom. Nick and Hildy sat on the bunk; Mr. Scott leaned back in the chair, against the locker.

"Nervous?" he asked them.

"A little," Nick said.

"Don't worry, Nick. You'll come through it all right. We're going to splash that battlewagon and make it back with a minimum of casualties. I'm sure of it."

"I hope so, Skipper," Hildy said.

"No matter what happens, keep calm. Remember that. You'll make good judgments. If you panic, you'll make mistakes."

"Yes, sir," Hildy said.

Nick's eyes fell on a photograph on Mr. Scott's desk. It was of Miss Snyder, in a civilian nurse's uniform.

"Her graduation picture," Mr. Scott said, noticing his interest. "She gave it to me after the dance."

"She's a swell girl," Hildy said.

"You'll be seeing more of her," Mr. Scott said. "After Okinawa, we'll be due for a few weeks of R and R — in Honolulu. She's going to finagle a way to join us."

"After R and R, what then, Skipper?" Nick asked.

"Japan. What else? That's all that'll be left."

"A long campaign?" Hildy said.

Mr. Scott shrugged his shoulders. "Before today, I would've guessed a year, maybe eighteen months. But after what that Jap pilot told Intelligence, I'm not sure."

Major Takamura had talked freely about conditions in his homeland, Mr. Scott told them. Even though General Tojo had resigned as premier, following the defeat at Saipan, the Army was still in firm control of the government. The Okinawa garrison, seventy-seven thousand troops, had been ordered to fight to the last man in order to delay the inevitable invasion of Japan. The garrison would be supported by massive kamikaze attacks, as many as forty-five hundred planes, on Task Force 58 and other American Naval forces. Japan still had plenty of ammunition and a deep reserve of aircraft — fifteen thousand at least. Ten thousand young men were training in the Kamikaze Corps, and more were volunteering. The Army would not admit defeat; the homeland would be defended inch by inch. In accordance with an Imperial General Headquarters directive, ammunition was being stockpiled in caves, tens of thousands of tons, as well as thousands of planes, which would be used in kamikaze crashes on American amphibious forces when the actual assault on Japan commenced. In addition, human kamikazes were being trained — young boys with firebombs, who would hurl themselves at American tanks. The government was rushing the production of two secret weapons. One was a human torpedo, called *kaiten,* which could be released from a submarine and guided to a target by its operator. The other was even more terrifying — a two-ton piloted suicide bomb, with rocket propulsion, that could attain speeds up to six hundred miles an hour and was almost impossible to shoot down. Emperor Hirohito wanted to end the war, Major Takamura had told Intelligence, but he was a virtual prisoner of the Army. Leaders who spoke of surrender were threatened with assassination.

"I think they're trying to wear us down," Mr. Scott said, "so that we'll accept a negotiated surrender favorable to their interests."

"Would you go along with that?" Nick asked him.

Mr. Scott passed around a pewter mug containing lemon drops and root beer balls.

"Would you?" he said. "After Pearl Harbor and Iwo and all the others?"

"No, sir," Nick replied, without hesitation. "Not for a minute."

He took a lemon drop and noticed that the mug bore the crest of Rutgers University.

"I didn't know you were at Rutgers, Mr. Scott."

"Just for a year," he said. "Before my appointment to Annapolis."

"What were you planning to major in?"

"Don't laugh," he said shyly. "Pre-med."

"I don't understand," Nick said. "From pre-med to the Naval Academy?"

"They're not incompatible professions, Nick," Mr. Scott said. "We're a defensive nation. If a professional military man does his job well, he can save a lot of lives." He looked at his watch. "Well, we'd better pack it."

"You're a philosopher," Nick said.

Mr. Scott smiled and stood up. "It's the war," he said. "War makes philosophers out of all of us. Good night, Nick. Hildy, how about a few games of acey-deucy tomorrow night?"

Hildy broke into a grin. "You're on, Skipper," he said. "I'll even spot you some points."

They made their way aft, through Damage Control and the CPOs' quarters, in the red glow of the battle lights that were turned on at night. Hildy was still grinning.

"He's a hell of a guy, isn't he?" he said. "One day he'll be an admiral, Nick, and we'll all be better for it."

11. SILENT MOVIES

TOMAINO WOKE THEM AT 0400, AN HOUR BE-fore GQ.

"What's for chow?" Hildy asked him, yawning.

"Steak and eggs."

"Fresh eggs or powdered?"

"Powdered."

Hildy frowned. "Powdered eggs, powdered milk,

powdered everything," he grumbled. "When I go to the head, all that comes out is powder."

"I'm taking along a couple of Baby Ruths," Tomaino said. "I nearly starved coming back yesterday. Hey, Enright. Up and at 'em."

"Okay, okay."

As Nick sat up, he banged his head on the bunk above him.

"Damn it," he muttered. "This compartment's a regular sardine can."

"You'd love it in a sub," Tomaino remarked. "The guys sleep between torpedoes."

In the ready room, after breakfast, the mood was subdued. Yesterday's briefing had been thorough; there was little to talk about. Hildy went up to the flight deck to check on the guns and the torpedo. Nick checked the weather data on the CIC printer. Winds from the southwest at eighteen knots; barometer at 29.43 and falling. Lousy weather. It would probably be overcast all the way to Honshu.

"Hey, O'Neal," he called across the room. "Have you been topside yet?"

"No, but Charlie has."

"How's the weather, Charlie?" Nick asked him.

"Soupy," he replied. "Do a good job on the radar. We don't want to drop those fish in Manchuria."

"Speaking of fish — " O'Neal said. "One time when the salmon were running in the Columbia River — " He was off on a story.

Nick glanced at the AVAILABILITY board. A full house. Raspberry Five was operational, and apparently Twelve had been patched up. They hadn't had 100 percent availability since the strikes on Chichi Jima. He wondered which names would be scratched when they got back.

RASPBERRY	PILOT	GUNNER/RADIOMAN	STATUS
		TORPEDO SQUADRON FORTY-THREE	
		Aircraft Availability	
DATE 19 March 1945		MISSION Yamato	
1	Scott	Hildebrandt/Enright	↑
2	Davison	Plummer/Melloy	↑
3	Herman	Couture/Bullock	↑
4	Tull	Serabia/Depew	↑
5	Lindblad	Bertrand/Bootz	↑
6	Parsons	Bromberg/Wilson	↑
7	Shong	Ponziani/Culpepper	↑
8	Bandy	Satchell/Nevins	↑
9	Werra	Jacob/Pfeiller	↑
10	Jones	Eichelberger/Pudvan	↑
11	Humboldt	Spilak/Middlesworth	↑
12	Riopelle	Butterfield/Farr	↑
13	Zito	Tomaino/Abraham	↑
14	Merz	Le Valley/Kipp	↑
15	Consiglio	O'Neal/Polovich	↑
16	Carpenter	Diskin/Shockley	↑

The printer began clattering with good luck messages from around the ship — CIC, the air officer, even the black gang, the men in the engine and boiler rooms. The one from Captain Rawlins drew a big laugh.

YAMATO GO BLOTTO ... GOOD LUCK, VT-43 ... YOUR CAPTAIN ...

Air Plot's was the most appropriate, Nick thought.

WILL BURN CANDLE IN WINDOW ... GODSPEED ... LT GOLDBERG ...

Nick was glad they were doing it by teletype and not in person. He was in no mood for speeches and stirring words of encouragement.

"All right, all right. Can the chatter and pay attention."

It was Mr. Scott, in his flight gear, at the blackboard.

"I want to remind all the radiomen that their torpedo arming levers may snap out of position if we encounter turbulence over the target. Make sure they're engaged. Sit on them, if you have to. We're not going to all this trouble just to drop a bunch of duds."

"Skipper," Barney said, "I picked up some strips of wire from the machinists. I'm going to wire my lever into place. I've got some spares."

He passed the lengths of wire to the other radiomen. Nick twisted his around his parachute harness. It would come in handy; the arming lever was tricky.

"Another thing — " Mr. Scott went on. "If you have to ditch on the way back, try to steer course zero-six-eight. Four submarines will be on 'lifeguard' patrol — the *Hackleback* and *Threadfin* and a couple others. So crank up your Gibson Girls. The subs will monitor the distress frequency for five minutes on the hour and again on the half-hour."

The Gibson Girl was the hand-cranked radio transmitter contained in a TBF's life raft packet, preset to an emergency frequency and with an antenna, in the form of a kite, that could be flown above the raft.

"I'd rather wait for a DD to pick us up," Ensign Consiglio said. "I'd get claustrophobia in one of those damn subs."

"What if our wristwatches get busted," Ensign Tull asked, "and we can't tell when it's the hour or half-hour?"

Mr. Scott smiled. "Then you'll do a lot of cranking," he said.

Everybody laughed.

"That's about all," Mr. Scott said. "Grab another sip of coffee while you can. We've got a lot of flying ahead of us."

The printer started clattering.

MOTHER GOOSE TURNING INTO WIND ...CLOUD COVER AT ANGELS THREE ...METEOROLOGY ADVISES POSSIBLE HEADWINDS ANGELS TEN 22 KNOTS... NEW VECTOR TO TARGET TWO-FOUR-FIVE MAGNETIC TWO-FOUR-EIGHT TRUE...

"Hey, Nick," Barney said, pulling an envelope from his pocket. "I forgot to show you these pictures. Remember that land I told you Loretta and I are going to buy?"

"On the Sangamon?"

"Yeah. Well, she's almost got enough money for the — "

The printer clattered again.

PILOTS AND CREWS MAN YOUR PLANES...

"Let's go, Nick," Barney said, putting on his red baseball cap. "I'll tell you about it when we get back."

The morning was gray and damp. Raspberry One was the first TBF into the air. Above the overcast, the rising sun cast an orange glow over the billowing clouds. The squadron rendezvoused at ten thousand feet and vectored north, maintaining a tight formation in order to concentrate the defensive firepower of the sixteen torpedo bombers. Slightly ahead of them, at fifteen thousand feet, their fighter escorts, thirty-four Hellcats, weaved back and forth across the pale blue sky. Twenty-five miles out, above the radar "pickets," the destroyers that formed the outer ring of the task force's defenses, there was a break in the cloud cover, but Nick could see that it was only a temporary clearing. Another cloud bank was visible on the northern horizon. By the time he picked up Kyushu on the radar, forty-five minutes into the mission, the overcast was solid again.

HILDY: Think the clouds will screw up our attack, Skipper?

MR. SCOTT: They might help, Hildy. We could stay above the cover till we're near the target, then drop down and begin our runs. If Nick gets a good fix on the anchorage, that is.

NICK: I'll do my best, Skipper.

MR. SCOTT: I know you will, Nick. How's our course?

NICK: I just picked up Kyushu. A correction four degrees to starboard should put us on a straight line to Tokyo.

MR. SCOTT: Roger, Nick. I hope the Japs are gullible.

The deceptive course was intended to trick the Japs into assuming that the attack would be on Tokyo or Yokohama; the vessels in the Inland Sea might be encouraged to relax their guard. The strike force would then abruptly veer west, toward Bungo Channel, the southwestern entrance to the sea. It would be Nick's responsibility to bring them in over the channel and steer them to Kure. The Imperial Fleet anchorage lay in the straits between a long, narrow island and the mainland. The surrounding terrain was rugged and mountainous. Raspberry One would need every ounce of power to get them out of there.

    MR. SCOTT: Bandits, Hildy! Ten o'clock high!
    HILDY: I see them, Skipper.
    NICK: Zekes?
    HILDY: Looks like a little of everything. Zekes, Oscars, Tojos. The Gumdrops will take care of them.
    MR. SCOTT: Charge your guns. Some of them might break through.

Hildy charged the turret gun and fired off a test burst to ensure that there was no jam. Nick did likewise with his stinger gun, then returned to the radar scope. He was getting good blips from Kyushu and from the southern tip of Shikoku. The dark space between the blips was Bungo Channel. They would have to change course in about twenty minutes. He glanced out the tiny port window. The sky above was filled with swirling vapor trails, like strands of white yarn flung at random, as the Gumdrops engaged the enemy planes in a wild melee. Air combat, viewed from the air, reminded Nick of a silent movie — pictures but no sound, just the steady drone of Raspberry One's engine. He lit a cigarette and watched the show. Six of the bandits — there were fifteen or twenty, he estimated — were in flames, but two of the Gumdrops were smoking and probably would have to ditch —

HILDY: Tojos! Three o'clock level!
MR. SCOTT: Where the hell did they come from?
HILDY: They sneaked in out of the sun.
MR. SCOTT: (radio) Raspberry Group, this is Raspberry One. Here they come. Tighten up the formation. Don't waste ammo. Wait till they're in range.

Nick ground out his cigarette and hunched over the stinger gun. Three greenish-brown, snub-nosed Tojos were attacking from five o'clock. The first pilot got careless, breaking off too soon and exposing his vulnerable underbelly. There was a quick burst from one of the TBFs. The Tojo rolled over and exploded.

HILDY: That was Tomaino. He finally gets on the SPLASH! board.

The entire squadron opened up on the other planes. The hail of tracers was so dense, it seemed that a glittering white beam was sweeping the sky. The second Tojo began smoking and went into a spin. The third one burst into flames but kept coming — straight at the four-plane section led by Raspberry One.

MR. SCOTT: (radio) Pull up! Pull up!

The TBFs nearly collided as they maneuvered out of the path of the flaming Tojo, which passed four feet below Raspberry One's tail wheel. Flames licked briefly at Nick's stinger bubble.

NICK: Whew! He came close enough to singe my eyebrows.

HILDY: You think he was trying to crash us, Skipper?

MR. SCOTT: He was probably dead, Hildy. The plane just kept flying.

A second wave of enemy planes jumped the strike force as it was vectoring to the west. Nick paid little attention to the attack; he was too busy giving Mr. Scott a good fix on Bungo Channel. The fighters quickly routed the attackers. The Jap planes, mostly Zekes this time, were no match for the Hellcats, and their pilots were clearly inexperienced. In two attacks, twenty-eight had been destroyed. But the Gumdrops were beginning to hurt. Eleven had had to ditch or abort; two had been shot down. As the TBFs neared the target, their fighter cover was down to twenty-three planes. Nick felt a fluttering in his stomach. The favorable tactical situation they had hoped for was deteriorating.

HILDY: Where the hell are these Japs coming from? We pulverized every airstrip in Kyushu yesterday.

MR. SCOTT: They're probably coming down from the north. Up around Nagamo. Maybe even Hokkaido.

HILDY: Swell.

The squadron had begun a gradual descent, throttling back so as to avoid building up speed. A torpedo run was tricky and hazardous. The torpedoes had to be aimed and dropped carefully, close to the target, the planes flying straight and steady and relatively slow, under two hundred knots. For thirty seconds, they would be sitting ducks, which is why the Gumdrops would be attacking simultaneously from a different direction, with rockets, to draw antiaircraft fire away from the exposed torpedo bombers.

> MR. SCOTT: (radio) Hello, Gumdrop Leader. This is Raspberry One. We're beginning our descent. Will level off at angels three. Over.
> GUMDROP LEADER: (radio) Roger, Raspberry One. We'll cover your descent, then swing around over Hiroshima and come in from the west. Good luck. Out.

They had cleared Bungo Channel and were now over the Inland Sea proper, which was sixty miles wide at this point, with many islands and Shinto religious shrines built out over the water. Nick checked the radar blips against the islands on his map. Oshima, Naka, Etajima, then the straits and the Naval installation at Kure, on the southeastern shore of Honshu. The bright blip coming from the anchorage was the *Yamato,* he was sure, but the smaller ones surrounding it puzzled him. Tugs and net-tenders, he assumed; the reconnaissance photos had shown a cruiser, probably the *Yahagi,* at the north end of the anchorage, the *Yamato* in the center, and a carrier and twelve destroyers well to the south.

> NICK: We're right on the button, Skipper. Range, six thousand yards.
> MR. SCOTT: Roger, Nick. We'll try to drop at five hundred yards. Everyone all set back there?
> HILDY: Roger.
> NICK: Roger.

MR. SCOTT: (radio) Raspberry Group, this is Raspberry One. Target dead ahead. Let's get on with it.

The TBFs dropped quickly through the clouds and fanned out. Nick grabbed the torpedo arming lever and glanced out the starboard window to confirm the accuracy of the radar fix. A blur of beauty slipped by below — green islands, blue water, prayer arches painted red and black, fishing villages with brown thatched roofs — reminding him of colored photographs he'd seen in the *National Geographic*. But something was wrong. The *Yahagi* was to the south, anchored near the carrier. The twelve destroyers were grouped around the *Yamato*. The bastards, he thought. They had rearranged the furniture.

MR. SCOTT: They've spotted us. Keep your fingers crossed.

The destroyers opened up first, then the *Yamato,* then the shore batteries, in a murderous barrage that made the sky look as though some giant hand had splattered mud at it. Two TBFs — Nick couldn't tell which ones — burst into flames and crashed into the water.

HILDY: Where the hell are the goddamn Gumdrops!

Nick could see where the Gumdrops were — at the south end of the anchorage, attacking the *Yahagi*. There had been a terrible miscalculation. Diving out of the clouds, they had been jumped by a pack of Zekes. Outnumbered and confused, they had mistaken the cruiser for the battleship. Now, as the Gumdrops maneuvered to correct their error, the Zekes were driving them even farther away from the *Yamato*. VT-43 was facing twelve destroyers and the world's greatest battleship — alone. Nick felt Raspberry One shudder from the concussion of an explosion and then smelled hydraulic fluid. He looked out both windows, trying to locate the hit.

MR. SCOTT: Where'd we get it, Nick?
NICK: Under the starboard wing. The landing gear's damaged, but it missed the gas tank.
MR. SCOTT: Smells like a hydraulic line's busted. I'm going to throw the bomb bay switch. See if the door opens.
NICK: Affirmative. Bomb bay door open.
MR. SCOTT: Okay. Arm the fish and call out the range.

Nick engaged the arming lever and secured it with Barney's wire.

NICK: Torpedo armed.

And as he did so, the plane was jarred by another concussion, but this time the hit wasn't for them. Through the port window he could see Raspberry Nine exploding in a great ball of fire. Something red sailed through the air. Barney's baseball cap. Farther back, two other Raspberries were in flames. He stared out the window, transfixed. None of it had any meaning for him yet. It was just a silent movie. The curtain would come down and the lights would go on, and everything would be all right —

MR. SCOTT: The range, Nick! Give me the range!
NICK: . . . one thousand yards . . . nine hundred
. . . eight . . seven . . six . . . five hundred yards
. . .
MR. SCOTT: Torpedo away! Let's get the hell out
of here!

There was a great roar as Mr. Scott gunned Raspberry One and pulled up over the *Yamato,* Nick and Hildy strafing the ship's quarter-deck and forward turrets, but causing little damage. The squadron's retreat vector was to the northwest, around Hiroshima, which lay in a valley. But the overcast was breaking up in that direction; sunlight had already spread over half the city. With the valley offering no cover, Mr. Scott banked full-power to the west, straining to clear a mountainous ridge and reach the safety of the clouds. Nick, through the stinger bubble, watched the track of the torpedo toward the *Yamato.* It had been a good drop, but the shore batteries were trying to blast the fish out of the water. They missed, but managed to deflect it. It veered around the *Yamato* toward a loading dock, where it blew up a tug and two patrol boats.

MR. SCOTT: (radio) Raspberry Group, this is
Raspberry One. Report! Report!
HILDY: There's no one to report, Skipper. They
all got shot down.
MR. SCOTT: (*pause*) Are you sure, Hildy?
HILDY: Yes, sir. Fifteen. I counted them.
MR. SCOTT: Did any of them get out?
HILDY: No, sir. They got shot to hell.
MR. SCOTT: What about the Gumdrops?

HILDY: They got it pretty bad, too. I saw six of them go down. They vectored to the south. They're probably low on fuel.

Mr. Scott didn't respond for several moments. They had cleared the ridge and were about two hundred feet from the clouds.

MR. SCOTT: Well, that sort of cuts down our options. But if we can sneak around Kyushu without getting jumped —
NICK: Zeke, Hildy! Zeke! Seven o'clock low.

Hildy's gun was pointed at two o'clock. A lone Zeke, effectively camouflaged against the foliage of the ridge, was in a climbing attack, out of range of Nick's gun. Hildy spun the turret around and blew up the Zeke with one short burst — but not before it had raked the forward area of Raspberry One's fuselage with gunfire.

MR. SCOTT: I'm hit . . .

Nick froze. Since their first combat mission, he had imagined all manner of horrible things happening to him and to Hildy, but never that Mr. Scott might be wounded.

NICK: Is it bad, Skipper?
MR. SCOTT: Bad enough.
NICK: Do you want to ditch?
MR. SCOTT: No . . . I think I can make it . . . It's hard for me to talk . . . Take over, Nick . . .

Communicate in questions . . . I'll click my mike
button once for 'yes,' twice for 'no' . . .

NICK: Yes, sir.

MR. SCOTT: One other thing . . . If I tell you to
bail out . . . don't argue . . .

NICK: Yes, sir.

Hildy slipped down from the turret and talked to
Nick off the intercom, half-shouting so that he could be
heard above the noise of the engine.

"We've got to do something, Nick. Get a first-aid
kit up to him or something."

"He's got a first-aid kit. Get back in the turret. The
Japs are all over the place."

"But it's not right, Nick." He seemed on the verge
of tears. "Him up there all alone . . . all shot up."

"Get back in the turret," Nick ordered him. "The
only thing we can do is help him keep this turkey in the
air."

Nick was amazed at his own composure. Quickly, he
checked the radar scope and his flight chart and came up
with a plan.

NICK: Level off just above the overcast, Skipper.
We'll cruise just above or just below the clouds,
depending on where the Japs are.

MR. SCOTT: *Click.*

NICK: Vector ten degrees port. That'll take us
over Bungo Channel. Kyushu is too risky.
They've probably patched up some of those airfields by now. They wouldn't see us, but they
might hear us and send up a few Zekes to in-
vestigate.

MR. SCOTT: *Click.*

Nick made a mental list of things to do. He would have to assess the damage to the landing gear and make sure the hook was down. Doc Boyd should be alerted — Air Plot would do that — and CIC would want a report. He was glad to be busy; it kept him from thinking. The torpedo attack still seemed unreal. All that mattered was making it back to the ship and getting medical attention for Mr. Scott. The shell holes in the fuselage had vented the plane of the odors of cordite and hydraulic fluid, but Nick had noticed a new smell, thick and sweet, and knew it was Mr. Scott's blood.

> HILDY: Bogeys at six o'clock, Nick. They're pretty far away. I don't think they've spotted us.
> NICK: Roger, Hildy. Skipper, we'd better duck under the clouds for a while.
> MR. SCOTT: *Click.*

Nick steered them through Bungo Channel and out over the ocean. Hildy scanned the sky from the turret, squinting against the bright sun and smoking one cigarette after another. They sighted bogeys five times, but managed to evade detection. Once, there were bogeys both above and below the clouds, which forced them to cruise straight through the gray, murky overcast. Thirty miles southeast of Kyushu, Nick worked out a new course, one that would keep them within Gibson Girl range of the lifeguard subs, in case they had to ditch. At 1012 hours, four hours into the mission, he picked up blips from the picket destroyers and relaxed a little. They were approaching friendly territory.

> NICK: (radio) Hello, Lancelot Control. Hello, Lancelot Control. This is Raspberry One, five-

five miles out at angels three, inbound for
Mother Goose. Over.
LANCELOT CONTROL: (radio) Roger, Raspberry
One. We have you on our scope. Mother Goose
bearing two-two-five, distance two-three miles.
Better hurry home. Lifeguard subs report bo-
geys, inbound from the northwest . . .

From Lancelot Control, Nick learned that four
Gumdrops had run out of fuel and ditched on the way
back; the remainder — thirteen planes — had landed
safely. CIC already had a combat report. The *Shiloh* was
steaming into the wind, recovering the CAP planes, which
were being armed for a second strike, intended to protect
the task force as it withdrew.

HILDY: The Gumdrops didn't do much better
than we did. I'll bet they're gloating in the Imperial Palace.

When Nick got a radar fix on the *Shiloh,* he ran
through the cockpit checklist for Mr. Scott — propeller
pitch to high, fuel mixture to rich, hook, flaps, landing
gear. The hook and flaps came down without difficulty,
but there was a problem with the landing gear. It would
lower but not retract, and Nick couldn't be sure whether
it was locked into position.

NICK: It might collapse when we hit the deck,
Skipper. Think you can handle it?
MR. SCOTT: *Click.*

But Nick was getting nervous. Mr. Scott was obviously growing weaker. His reactions were jerky and

uncertain. We'd better hurry, Nick thought. He switched his mike to VHF and hoped that Lieutenant Goldberg was on duty in Air Plot. He was.

NICK: (radio) Hello, Mother Goose. Hello, Mother Goose. This is Raspberry One, ten miles out at bearing zero-four-five, descending from angels three. Request immediate emergency landing. Over.

MOTHER GOOSE: (radio) Roger, Raspberry One . . . Is that you, Commander Scott?

NICK: (radio) Negative. Commander Scott is wounded. This is Nick Enright, the radioman.

MOTHER GOOSE: (radio) We're going to have to land you in the drink, Nick. We have seven more CAPs to recover, and then we're turning out of the wind. There are bogeys in the area. Suggest you pick out a destroyer and ditch alongside her . . .

Nick's heart sank. He understood the priorities of the decision. There were three thousand men in the *Shiloh* to be protected, only three in Raspberry One. But for them it was a death sentence. The TBF was an easy plane to ditch — as long as the landing gear was retracted. With the gear down, the plane would flip over on its back and sink with the crew trapped inside.

NICK: (radio) We've got a problem, Mother Goose. Our landing gear is down and won't retract.

MOTHER GOOSE: (radio) Oh . . . (*pause*) . . . Stand by, Raspberry One —

Mr. Scott's voice came on the intercom, so weak it was scarcely audible. There was a gurgling sound in his throat.

> MR. SCOTT: I'll climb to five thousand . . . You bail out . . .
> HILDY: Nothing doing, Skipper. We're in this to the end. Together.
> MOTHER GOOSE: (radio) Raspberry One, is Commander Scott capable of making a straight-in approach?
> MR. SCOTT: *Click*.
> NICK: (radio) Affirmative, Mother Goose.
> MOTHER GOOSE: (radio) Roger. Stand by . . . (*pause*) . . . Attention all CAP Hellcats in the pattern. Climb to angels two and hold. We have an emergency landing . . . Okay, Raspberry One. You're cleared. Just one pass, so make it good.
> NICK: (radio) Thanks, Mr. Goldberg.

The *Shiloh* was only five miles away now, steaming in rough seas. Nick worried about Mr. Scott's vision; it might be weak and unsteady. He ordered Hildy to swing the turret forward, pointed at the landing signals officer's platform, and call out the LSO's instructions.

> HILDY: . . . Right in the groove, Skipper . . . A little low; bring it up . . . That's it . . . Watch the airspeed . . . More throttle! More throttle! We're going to stall! . . . That's better . . . The deck's pitching like hell, so watch it . . . Just a hundred yards now, Skipper . . . Bring it down a little . . . Okay, CUT!

Raspberry One settled to a perfect landing. The hook caught the third arresting wire. Nick braced himself for the possible collapse of the landing gear. The port one held; the starboard gear snapped like a toothpick. The plane careened down the deck, coming to a stop above a port gun gallery. The starboard wing was sheared off, and the hatch to the radio compartment was jammed shut. It took the deck crew several minutes to pry it open.

"*Clear the deck!*" Captain Rawlins called from the bridge, through a bullhorn. "*We've got aircraft to recover!*"

The deck was a scene of confusion. The ship was at general quarters. The CAP fighters were holding at five hundred feet, low on fuel. The 40-millimeter guns were elevated and trained; the 20s were firing test bursts. A deck crane was moving toward Raspberry One. Nick and Hildy piled out of the radio compartment, uninjured. Doc Boyd was climbing down from the stub of the starboard wing. The Protestant chaplain was with him.

"Mr. Scott!" Hildy hollered, and started to climb up on the wing stub. "We're coming!"

Doc Boyd grabbed him.

"He's dead, Hildy," he said. "He bled to death."

Hildy looked at him in disbelief.

"What do you mean, he's dead?" he said. "He just landed this goddamn airplane, didn't he?"

The emergency siren was wailing from the bridge. The crane had moved into position. Two plane handlers were looping a cable around the plane. Hildy tried to grab the cable from them.

"You leave that plane alone!" he shouted. "You're not going to dump him like a hunk of garbage!"

Doc Boyd pulled him away.

"There's no time, Hildy. The kamikazes are out. They've already hit the *Wasp*."

The crane swung Raspberry One out over the water, the TBF dangling like a crumpled pendant. Mr. Scott's body was slumped forward in the cockpit. Nick noticed that the canopy was splattered with blood. The cable was released, and the once-proud torpedo bomber hit the water, nose first, and started to sink.

"Oh, Jesus Christ goddamn son of a bitch!" Hildy cried, in tears, and started running down the deck.

"Go after him, Nick," Doc said. "I've got to stand by for the CAP landings."

Hildy was heading for the starboard catwalk, the ready room, Nick assumed.

"Hildy!" he yelled, running after him. "Wait for me!"

The antiaircraft batteries had opened up on something. Nick tripped on an arresting wire. As he picked himself up, there was a great explosion behind him. Shrapnel and debris were shooting into the air. He felt something spin him around, like a dull blow, but he remained on his feet. A cloud of black smoke engulfed him, and a glob of oil or grease hit his forehead. When he tried to wipe it away, it seemed to get wetter — and he discovered that his right arm had no hand. He stared dumbly at the tattered wrist — the splinters of bone, the strands of muscle, the blood gushing from a torn vein. He'd never seen the inside of an arm before. How cleverly it was put together. He'd have to stop the bleeding, of course. Barney Jacob was good at first aid; he would fix it —

There were more explosions, a string of them, like firecrackers. God, it was noisy. And smoky. He noticed

Hildy running back toward him. His Mae West was ripped, and blood was streaming down his face. A nosebleed, probably. Barney would fix that, too —

"Doc!" Hildy screamed. "Come quick! It's Nick!"

12. Duck Shorts and Floppy Hats

IT WAS THREE DAYS BEFORE THE SEQUENCE of destruction was pieced together. The final Action Report attributed the success of the kamikazes to the fact that the *Shiloh* was in the process of recovering aircraft, which made it impossible for radar operators to distinguish between friendlies and bogeys; and to the overcast skies, which prevented visual spotting of the Judys — there were eight — until they were diving out of the clouds. Even so, the ship's alert gunnery crews destroyed four of them before the explosions. Many gunners died at their posts, at the handlebars of the 20s or in the farm-tractor seats of the 40s, killed by their own ammunition, which exploded in the intense heat. Casualties were also high among the flight deck crews, boys not old enough to shave — butchered by exploding aircraft or incinerated in the flames or blown into the sea to face the sharks. Mutilated flesh littered the deck like offal, and the scuppers ran red with blood.

The first kamikaze, already in flames from the marksmanship of the gunners, crashed onto the flight deck forward of Number 2 elevator, in an area where twelve second-strike F6Fs, armed with Tiny Tim rockets, were being fueled. Its thousand-pound bomb penetrated to the hangar deck, where it went off in a gigantic blast that twisted the elevator like taffy and set fire to the second-strike Hellcats. A great column of flames and debris and human limbs shot three hundred feet into the air. Fuel lines ruptured, and burning gasoline washed down into the gun galleries. It was flying shrapnel from this explosion that severed Nick's hand and lacerated Hildy's face.

"Doc! Come quick! It's Nick!"

Doc Boyd saw immediately that the port boatswain's gallery, forward of the LSO's platform and under the lip of the flight deck, might escape the flames.

"The boatswain's gallery!" he shouted to Hildy. "It's our only chance!"

He and Hildy ran toward the port catwalk, carrying Nick between them. Blood gushed from Nick's arm and from the jagged laceration on the left side of Hildy's face. The ship was an inferno of flames and gunfire. Shrapnel rained down everywhere — and torn bodies. Doc tripped on a human head that rolled across the deck; Hildy grabbed him and kept him from falling overboard. The sky was black with ack-ack bursts, but the kamikazes kept coming. A second one crashed behind them, but they reached the safety of the gallery before its bomb exploded.

"Plasma!" Doc hollered to a corpsman. "Plasma!"

Hildy unbuckled Nick's flight gear — harness, Mae West, gun belt — then tore off his own dungaree and skivvy shirts, tying the skivvy around his face to staunch the bleeding. Doc ripped off Nick's right sleeve and took a syringe of morphine from his black bag.

"I've got to carve a flap out of your wrist, Nick!" he shouted above the explosions. "The morphine will help, but it's going to hurt!"

But Nick wasn't listening. He was staring in horror

out over the water. The fin of a shark was moving toward
a boy who'd been blown overboard. The boy was struggling to cling to a piece of floating debris. It was over in
a few seconds. A flailing of arms, a wild thrashing — then
nothing. Nick grabbed Hildy and pulled him close.

"Hildy . . ." he said weakly. "Are we going to sink?"

"I don't know, Nick."

"If we go down . . . take my thirty-eight and shoot
me . . . I don't want the sharks to get me . . ."

"Don't worry, Nick," Hildy said. "I'll shoot the
sharks."

Doc slipped a wooden tongue-depressor between
Nick's teeth.

"Bite on it, Nick," he said. "Hard."

The rest was a blur. Nick was in a stupor when Doc
put his sutured arm into a sling fashioned out of Hildy's
dungaree shirt.

"Keep it elevated, Nick," he shouted into his ear.
"Do you hear me? It's an extremity. It'll burst open under
pressure. Keep it elevated."

Nick nodded dully. Hildy rushed off to help with the
fires; Doc turned to the other wounded men who had been
dragged to the gallery. Nick felt himself fading away.
His arm hurt horribly. The gallery was getting hot from
the fires in the hangar deck, which made him feel better.
The sharks wouldn't get him; he would fry to death.
Like an egg. He would love an egg . . . with slices of crisp
scrapple . . . *"Breakfast is ready, son"* . . . *"Coming, Dad"*
. . . and then he would sit at his bedroom window and
watch the snow falling over the square . . . cool, lovely
snow . . . He passed out.

The *Shiloh* took four kamikazes within ninety seconds. The second one, diving from port, crashed near the

barrier. Its bomb, too, exploded in the hangar deck, turning it into an inferno that wiped out everyone working there. The third cartwheeled across the flight deck and blew up on the port catwalk. Its bomb exploded fourteen feet under water, ripping the *Shiloh*'s hull in several places. The ship began to take on sea water, first in a gurgle, then in a gush. The last Judy, in a ninety-degree dive, crashed directly amidships. Its bomb, with a delayed-action fuse, tore through four decks, detonating above the engine and boiler rooms. There were now fires in every deck, fed by aviation gasoline pouring down from above.

The *Shiloh* had been organized to withstand enemy bombs — within limits. When the attack began, the ship's six hundred watertight compartments were closed and dogged. Damage control parties, repair parties, fire fighting crews — all were standing by at strategic locations throughout the ship. The battle dressing stations were also ready, manned by teams of doctors, pharmacist's mates, and hospital corpsmen, who worked without letup in the heat and smoke — injecting drugs, applying tourniquets, dressing burns, administering plasma, sulfa, and penicillin, suturing wounds, amputating shredded limbs. The most critically wounded were successfully evacuated to the *Shawnee*, whose skipper slammed the cruiser alongside the exploding carrier and held her with his engines while the casualties were being lowered. A dozen ships — destroyers, cruisers, battleships — had moved quickly to form a protective ring around the *Shiloh*, still fighting off the Japanese attack, which continued through the day and into the night.

But it seemed doubtful that even the vast resources of Task Force 58 could save the ravaged carrier, which was now being wracked by internal explosions that knocked out her boilers and fire mains. Within two hours, all way was lost, and the great ship lay dead in the water, without electrical power or communications, listing dangerously to port. The *Abilene*, Admiral Lawton's flagship, and three destroyers moved close to the *Shiloh* from starboard, leeward to the flames. The admiral, through a bullhorn, called across the water to Captain Rawlins.

"We are standing by to pick up survivors. Suggest you prepare your men to abandon ship."

Captain Rawlins, on the signal bridge, his forehead bloodied and his khaki uniform streaked with oil, grabbed a bullhorn from his executive officer.

"In a pig's ass!" he bellowed to the admiral. "We're keeping this lady afloat!"

If there was a turning point in the *Shiloh*'s ordeal, a point at which the battered crew came to believe in the impossible, it was the ring of conviction in the captain's salty response to Admiral Lawton. He asked the *Abilene* to stand by with a towline, then made his way belowdecks, through the dense smoke and scorching heat, to help Number 4 fire crew, which was fighting to get through to the damaged engine rooms so that power could be restored to the fire mains. Without power, the ship was doomed; with it, there was a chance. The sight of their captain manning a hose boosted the spirits of the blistered, half-suffocated men as they battled the flames with foam extinguishers and mobile water pumps powered by gasoline engines — the deck slick with oil, sea water, and blood; the bulkheads so hot, flesh sizzled when brushed against them. Behind them, the damage control and repair parties moved in swiftly, with battle lanterns and hand flashlights, plugging and shoring the breaks in the hull, using acetylene torches to free men trapped under twisted steel; stringing emergency lighting from auxiliary generators, rigging blowers to suck out the smoke, repairing battle telephones.

By 1530 hours, the ship had begun to regain power. The *Abilene* passed a towline and hauled the listing carrier around to a southerly course, away from the threat of enemy attack, making six knots. By 1630, with the mains restored, all fires were reported under control. Three hours later, with darkness spreading over the now-calm waters of the China Sea, the boilers were capable of delivering ten knots. The towline was cast off, and the *Shiloh,* still smoking but its list corrected to thirteen degrees, proceeded under its own power. Admiral Lawton flashed a message, by blinker: WELL DONE, *SHILOH.*

The message was repeated three times, the cruiser abeam the *Shiloh,* within view of the port boatswain's gallery. Nick, weak from loss of blood and his mind dulled by morphine, saw the blinking light and instinctively read the Morse code. Slowly, unbelievingly, he comprehended its meaning. The ship was not going to sink.

"You'll be okay now, buddy," a corpsman said as he removed the rubber tube that had been dripping plasma into Nick's left arm. "A lot of other guys need this stuff."

Nick had lain in the gallery for nine hours, with thirty other wounded men — feverish, at times delirious, the sutured stump of his right arm throbbing with excruciating pain — unaware of the struggle below-decks to save the ship, fully expecting to die, afraid that Hildy was already dead.

"I stashed your gun and stuff in a coil of rope," the corpsman said, helping Nick to his feet. "I hate to kick you out, but we need the space. You can walk around, if you feel up to it. Doc Boyd'll check that arm soon's he can. He's doing surgery on the fantail."

It was a black, moonless night. The corpsman boosted Nick up a short ladder to the flight deck, which resembled a smoldering battlefield — strewn with shrapnel and the twisted frames of aircraft, the barrier gone, the bomb holes still smoking. Nick was reminded of a remark someone had made about Iwo Jima — that it looked like hell with the fire out. A work party moved like specters in the ashen light of battle lanterns, preparing the dead for burial. Other than casualties viewed from the air, Nick had seen only two dead persons before — his paternal grandfather and a boy at St. Luke's, in the eighth grade, who'd been run down by a car. The boy's head had been crushed, but they had fixed him up, and at the funeral home he looked peaceful and reposed. There had been no time for such amenities on the flight deck. Long rows of corpses lined the port edge of the deck, wrapped in canvas and weighted with bars of lead, the canvas and lead having been transferred from the other ships. Some were just torsos; the limbs had been blown away. The remains of others had been scraped from the deck and deposited in seabags. On each bag was an identification tag. Nick thought he saw a familiar name on one tag. He asked a seaman to flash his lantern on it: 880-65-70, GOLDBERG, AARON, D., LT., USNR.

The bag seemed almost empty. He stared at the tag, remembering. *"The management and staff welcome you to the* Shiloh." He should have gone down to Air Plot weeks ago and introduced himself.

The burial service was about to begin. Nick saw Doc Boyd climbing up from the starboard catwalk and went over to see him. The front of his khaki uniform was drenched with blood from the surgery he'd performed.

"You should get off your feet," he said to Nick. "You lost a lot of blood."

"I'm okay," Nick said. "Is Hildy alive?"

"He's below-decks," Doc said, "with the repair crews. A little banged up, but nothing serious." He surveyed the charred flight deck. "God, what a holocaust."

No one knew why the ship was still afloat, he said, but it was, and they'd been ordered back to the States for repairs. To New York; the West Coast Navy Yards were jammed. The wounded would remain aboard, all who were able to make the trip. Captain Rawlins said it would be the best medicine for them. They were steaming now toward a rendezvous with an oiler. They'd lost a lot of fuel oil, which was one of the causes of the list. He pressed a hand to Nick's forehead.

"Your fever's down," he said. "Infection is the big worry. I've got to check on my patients on the fantail. I'll take a closer look at you later."

Captain Rawlins had come on deck, scarcely recognizable, his uniform was so torn and dirty. All men who were able to move gathered around him, facing the rows of canvas shrouds. Nick felt wobbly. He stayed off to starboard, leaning against the funnel.

"For as much as it has pleased Almighty God to take out of the world the souls of our departed shipmates . . ."

Nick thought it odd that neither of the chaplains was there. Maybe they were dead. Death was everywhere — and the lingering stench of burning flesh. It had permeated his clothes, soaked into his pores. He could feel it, taste it.

". . . looking for the life eternal, when the moaning

sea shall give up her dead, and there shall be no more sea . . ."

As the captain's words drifted into the black night, Nick saw flashes of gunfire ripple across the horizon and heard the rumble. The Japs were still trying to break through and finish off the *Shiloh*. The bastards, he thought. The dirty bastards.

". . . Ad Deum qui laetificat juventutem meam . . ."

A montage of mourning, a kind of reverent babble, rose from the gathered men, hesitantly, awkwardly — prayers, chants, hymns — in choir-boy soprano, altar-boy Latin, bar-mitzvah Hebrew.

". . . In the sweet bye and bye . . . Y'heh sh'meh rabbo m'vorach . . . I am the Resurrection and the life . . . Quia tu es, Deus, fortitudo mea . . . he who believes in Me, even if he die, shall live . . ."

There was more gunfire, this time a barrage of it. Nick felt an anger building in him, a hatred. They'd given it to the Japs often enough, true; but they had asked for it. It was their war, and they could quit whenever they wanted. Playground bullies, that's all they were. That's what the whole war really boiled down to, he supposed; bullies trying to push other people around — Tojo, Hitler, Mussolini, all of them. At some point, you had to make a stand, but, God, it was hard. The bloodshed, the suffering, the destruction. Whatever the Japs got in return, it wouldn't be enough . .

". . . Rock of Ages, cleft for me . . ."

He thought of the warriors of the ages, famous units that had fought to the death, and felt a strong kinship with them. The Spartans at Thermopylae, the Light Brigade at Balaclava, Custer rallying his men for a last stand at the Little Bighorn. And now VT-43 in the Inland Sea. The Japs on the *Yamato* were probably toasting each

other with sake and bragging about all the American torpedo bombers they'd shot down.

"...*Let me hide myself in Thee* ..."

But the squadron wasn't finished yet — not quite. He
and Hildy were still alive. He had his .38; Hildy had his
knife. They would slip away in one of the life rafts that
were lashed to the hull below the island. Several were undamaged; he'd seen them. The Inland Sea couldn't be
too far. The ocean currents would carry them most of the
way. They'd need a motor to get back, of course, but that
was no problem. They could pick up a used Evinrude at
Cape May, at Eddie's bait shack, up the beach from his
family's summer cottage. Eddie would let them have it
on credit. He smiled inwardly. The Japs would never
expect an attack by life raft ...

"You look shaky, Nick." It was Doc Boyd with a
hypo. "I'm going to give you another shot, and then let's
find a place where you can crap out. Maybe one of the
gun galleries."

It was all very clear in his mind. Hildy would rig a
bomb or something; he was good at improvising. They
would blow up the *Yamato* and escape in the smoke and
confusion. Franny and Diane would be waiting for them
when they got back, on the pier at Eddie's, in duck shorts
and floppy straw hats. "What a funny boat," Franny
would say, laughing, and they would all hike up the beach
to a seafood place ... Franny talking excitedly about the
kamikaze that had washed up in the rocks at Wickford
... Diane and Hildy romping in the sand like cats ...

"... *Gloria Patri, et Filio, et Spiritui Sancto* ..."

They would drink beer and eat clams and dance barefoot to the music of the jukebox, swaying to the —

"... *We commit their bodies to the deep.*"

He fell asleep counting the splashes.

13. Cloth Sacks

IN THE MORNING, WITH THE SUN RISING
gold and lovely over the blue Pacific, as in a travel poster,
the great carrier — gutted, blackened from the smoke of
battle, but its tattered ensign flying and its boilers producing fifteen knots — set course for the Panama Canal.

"Now hear this," the captain's voice boomed out
when the loudspeaker system was working again. "This
ship is a goddamn mess. All hands turn to."

And the crew, what was left of it — dazed, exhausted,
hurting — set about making the ship habitable for the
long voyage home, restoring the evaporators and the
heads, firing up the ovens, jettisoning the debris, inven-
torying the ship's critical needs — stores, medicine, re-
placement equipment, repairs — which would be supplied
by the logistics support group in a day or two. By 0700
hours, coffee and bread, day old, were available. Hildy,
limping badly, took some to Number 3 gun gallery, just
aft of the funnel, where Nick had spent the remainder of
the night, curled up against a 40-millimeter gun mount,
on his right side so that his stump would be elevated.

"How's the arm, Nick?" he said, nudging him.

"Manageable," Nick said, and yawned.

"Do you want Doc to give you another shot?"

"No. That stuff makes me groggy." He sat up and
started to rub his eyes with his right arm; the sling reminded him that the arm had no hand. "What'd you do to
your leg?"

"It's my knee," Hildy said. "I wrenched it down on
Three Deck. I was helping the fire crews."

The gun gallery had been mangled by exploding

rockets. Hildy kicked aside some shrapnel and slumped down next to Nick. He was still bare to the waist, his hands and arms blistered with burns, his shoulders a mass of purple bruises. The gash on his face had been bandaged.

"How many stitches did it take?" Nick asked him.

"Thirty. One of the dentists sewed it up."

"Painful?"

"Only when I smile. So don't make me laugh."

"What's there to laugh about?" Nick said. "How many guys did we lose?"

"They're not sure. Doc says six hundred, probably more. I guess the sharks got a lot of them."

Nick took a swallow of the hot coffee. Some of it dribbled down his chin.

"I'll have to practice," he said. "I'm not used to drinking with my left hand."

"You were lucky." Hildy lit two cigarettes and handed him one. "We were both lucky."

"I know," Nick said. The first drag from the cigarette made him dizzy. "After seeing that gore on the flight deck, losing a hand is like stubbing a toe."

They sat in silence for a while, drinking the coffee and eating the dry bread, their first food since the battle breakfast of the previous morning.

"Tastes good," Nick said.

"Yeah," Hildy said. He leaned over and peered closely at some reddish specks in Nick's hair.

"What's that crud in your hair?"

"I got splattered by someone's insides," Nick said. "I thought I'd gotten it all out."

"It's starting to stink." Hildy got to his feet. "They've got fresh water down on Two Deck. I'll get a bucket."

"You'd better stay off that leg."

"It's nothing," Hildy said. "Can you make it to the ready room?"

"I think so."

"That's where we'll be bunking. Our compartment got burned out. I scrounged a couple of mattresses and some towels from the CPOs' quarters."

Fire had swept through the ready room too, erasing every trace of the warm squadron life that had once filled it — the SPLASH! board, the funny cartoons, Doc Boyd's restorative cabinet with its *Tables for Ladies* sign. But it was in better shape than most of the ship and offered accessibility to the catwalk, where Nick and Hildy could drag their mattresses when the ship neared the equator and the nights grew hot. Besides, the ready room was VT-43 country; they felt they belonged there, and no one questioned their occupancy. The entire ship's company was making do as best it could — scavenging soap, toothbrushes, bedding; contriving billets wherever the damage allowed, like squatters.

"I'm beginning to appreciate what London went through during the blitz," Nick remarked.

On the day the *Shiloh* rendezvoused with the support group, Captain Rawlins, his forehead bandaged where a fragment of the first kamikaze had grazed it, paid a visit to the ready room to inform them of administrative changes involving the air group and to express his condolences.

"Best damn torpedo squadron in the fleet," he said, chewing on a cigar. "Commander Scott was in line to command one of the new air groups forming at North Island."

He had special words of praise for Hildy, which was

how Nick learned that Hildy had saved the lives of three hundred men trapped in the suffocating smoke of a pitch-black mess compartment. With a battle lantern and an ax, he had led them to safety, injuring his knee when he went back to help a hysterical mess boy whose face had been blown away and who was choking to death on his own blood.

"You kept the ship afloat, son," Captain Rawlins said, shaking Hildy's hand. "I mean it. You and men like you."

CAG 43, he told them, had been decommissioned. The CAP pilots who made it to the *Bennington* had been reassigned to that carrier's air group, as had Dr. Boyd, who would leave the ship when they anchored briefly at Ulithi. Nick and Hildy were now ship's company. When the *Shiloh* docked in New York, around April 19, they would be transferred to a hospital in Brooklyn, not far from the Navy Yard. Meanwhile, they would be under the supervision of the medical officer, to whom they would submit a list of personal items lost or damaged in the fires — uniforms, toilet articles, dungarees — which would be replaced by a stores ship. As he was leaving, Captain Rawlins had a word of sympathy.

"I know what you're going through," he said. "I was on the *Hornet* when Torpedo Eight got it, at Midway. If you need a shoulder to cry on, my door is always open."

When the captain had gone, Nick looked at Hildy in amazement.

"That mess boy," he said. "Did he make it?"

"I think so."

"What'd you do?"

"Some tissue was blocking his windpipe. I cut it away with my hunting knife."

"Oh, God," Nick said, feeling sick.

Hildy's activities explained the stream of well-wishers who had begun to appear at the ready room, many of them bearing tokens of gratitude — an acey-deucy board, playing cards, two chairs and a navigation table salvaged from Air Plot.

"Not a bad haul," Hildy remarked as their acrid lodgings took on a more pleasant character. "Now, if someone would just scrounge a radio that's still working."

Someone did, and at night, with a breeze coming in off the catwalk, Hildy would tune in Tokyo Rose, a favorite with the fleet because of her hilarious propaganda and the Glenn Miller records she played. One night, after announcing the sinking of the *Shiloh*, she played "Moonlight Serenade."

"If I shut my eyes," Hildy said, "I can see the casino and hear the water lapping on Narragansett Bay."

At first, Nick felt uncomfortable, sharing the benefits of Hildy's heroism — especially when a shipfitter with bandaged arms spent an hour hooking up a reading lamp next to his mattress. But it soon became evident that the acts of sympathy were tributes not just to Hildy, but to the entire squadron. The *Shiloh*'s casualty ratio had been devastating; VT-43's, numbing — forty-six dead and one wounded out of a roster of forty-eight. And when Doc Boyd laid eyes on Hildy's knee, which had swollen to twice its normal size, the ratio became a clean sweep.

"Stay off that leg," he ordered him. "It'll require surgery."

He requisitioned a wooden splint and a pair of crutches from the medical supplies taken aboard from the support group. It was necessary to slit Hildy's trouser leg, then secure the seam with large safety pins.

"You won't win any fashion awards," Doc said, "but it should hold you till you get back to the States."

Doc Boyd's last responsibility before leaving the ship was to collect the effects of the VT-43 dead. They would be mailed to each man's next of kin, along with a letter of condolence. He asked Nick to help.

"Will you write the letters?" Nick asked him.

"No. Captain Rawlins. He insisted on it."

In the aircrewmen's compartment, the bunks had been destroyed, but one tier of lockers had been only scorched, and the contents were relatively undamaged.

"Just personal things, Nick," Doc said, handing him a pile of little cloth sacks. "Watches, rings, photographs, letters — that sort of thing. Destroy any dirty pictures or salacious material. And scan the letters to make sure there's nothing embarrassing in them. We don't want to break a wife's heart by sending her a torrid love letter her husband received from some floozy in Providence."

It was slow going for Nick, but he welcomed the opportunity to practice doing routine things with his left hand. He still couldn't fully accept the fact that they were gone — Barney Jacob, O'Neal, Charlie Wilson, Tomaino. And sifting through the mementoes of their brief lives — class rings, 4-H ribbons, pictures of pretty girls in pleated skirts and saddle shoes — it seemed that at any moment the arresting gear would start whanging, and they would come trooping down to the ready room, tired, sweaty, talking excitedly about the mission. He went through Barney's things cautiously, hoping there'd be nothing indiscreet. There wasn't. A picture of Barney's wife was propped up on the top shelf, a portrait in a small leather frame. He would go visit her, Nick decided — and Mr. Scott's parents, too. It might help them, to talk to someone from the squadron. He thought of how Barney's wife had looked that night at Penn Station, waving from the platform with the baby in her arms — so young, so vulnerable. What would she do now?

"She's a lovely girl," Doc Boyd said, peering over his shoulder. "Like a Dresden doll. She brightened our house when she stayed with us at Quonset Point."

"I know," Nick said. "Hildy and I met her on the train."

The picture slipped from his hand. As he leaned over to pick it up, his stump banged against the locker door. He shuddered from the pain.

"Is it still throbbing?" Doc asked him.

"Yes, sir," Nick said, afraid he was going to pass out. "Sometimes it feels as if it's going to explode."

"It will ease up in a week or so," Doc said. "Aside from the pain, how are you adjusting to your new circumstances?"

"All right, I guess." Nick shrugged. "Of course, it sort of puts a crimp in my romantic plans."

"Why should it? I met Franny only once, but she's a strong girl. You sense it in her. She won't bat an eye."

"Maybe not," Nick said. "But I will."

"Self-pity is deadly to an amputee, Nick. We're all handicapped, in one way or another. Physically, emotionally, intellectually. Yours happens to show. That's the only difference. Remember that."

"I'll try to, Doc," Nick said. "Right now, I'm not thinking too clearly. I haven't even remembered to thank you. Without you, one of these sacks would be for me."

"Don't thank me," Doc said. "Thank Hildy. If he hadn't yelled when he did, there'd be a sack for me, too.

I was standing in the exact spot that the second kamikaze hit."

He took a small notebook from his pocket and wrote something in it.

"We may as well say good-by now, Nick," he said. "We'll be anchoring at Ulithi at eighteen hundred. Here's my address in North Platte. Stay in touch. There aren't many of us left."

"I will, Doc," Nick promised, feeling a great warmth for this gentle man who had saved his life. "Maybe one day we'll hoist a few restoratives at the Big Horn Saloon."

"God bless you, Nick." Doc smiled and shook Nick's left hand. "It's funny about war. It's rotten, but you meet a lot of nice people along the way."

That night, under a star-filled sky, having taken on additional hospital corpsmen and eighty-six canvas cots, which had been requisitioned directly by Captain Rawlins, the *Shiloh* resumed her voyage, escorted by two destroyers, an oiler, and two light cruisers, the *Ann Arbor* and the *Terre Haute*. The vessels maintained a diamond formation around the crippled carrier, with the cruisers at the forward and aft points. Strolling on the flight deck, Nick could see the other ships in the moonlight. It was lovely, he thought, not having to worry about kamikazes.

While at Ulithi, Captain Rawlins had completed the casualty list, which was posted in various parts of the ship. Nick was stunned. Seven hundred and fourteen killed or missing, and two hundred and sixty-five wounded, over a hundred of them critically — the ones who had been lowered to the *Shawnee* while the fires raged. CINCPAC issued a bulletin from Guam, declaring the toll to be the worst of the Pacific campaign. The bulletin praised "the outstanding skill, stamina, and heroism" of the *Shiloh*'s crew, and noted that in the annals of sea warfare, no capital ship had ever sustained such severe damage and remained afloat.

"The guys the sharks are digesting will be pleased to learn that," Hildy said dryly — and Nick looked at him in surprise. He'd never heard Hildy make a cynical remark before.

A memorial service was scheduled for the following Sunday, with the names of those killed to be read by representatives of the various ship's company divisions with which they'd served. The Protestant chaplain, who had lost an eye in an explosion below-decks (Father O'Rourke had been killed while trying to drag a steward's mate to safety, in the wardroom), asked Nick if he would read a passage from Scripture when the names of the VT-43 dead were called out.

"Something from Revelation," he said. "Toward the end of the service. It will be very brief. I've asked Hildy to read the names."

The service was held at sunset, on the flight deck, which had been cleared of debris. The gaping bomb holes were boarded over; the twisted Number 2 elevator cordoned off. Able-bodied members of the crew, in dress whites, stood at attention abaft the island, leaning forward slightly against the list of the ship, which had been corrected substantially but was still at six degrees. There were remarks by the chaplain and by Captain Rawlins. Then the names, read to the rolling of drums. And the prayers, in boyish voices — psalms, the mourner's Kaddish, supplications from the Bible.

"They that go down to the sea in ships, that do business in great waters . . ."

And as the drums rolled and the hundreds of names droned out over the charred flight deck, the magnitude of the disaster that had befallen his ship, his squadron, hit Nick with a deadening impact.

> ". . . these see the works of the Lord, and His wonders in the deep."

It seemed a bad dream. He was only nineteen years old. He should be at Princeton, drinking beer and singing fight songs; reading Shakespeare and studying the Greek philosophers. Instead, he had participated in a great killing of human beings. Hundreds? Thousands? Once a trigger was pressed or a bomb released, who could say? Enemies committed to killing him, true; but that didn't make it any easier to live with. When it was his turn to read, his voice cracked, and a profound sorrow welled up in him.

> "And God shall wipe away all tears from their eyes; and there shall be no more death, neither sorrow, nor crying."

A bugle sounded taps. The chaplain read a benediction. The service ended. Nick, his eyes blurred with tears, hurried from the flight deck, avoiding Hildy, avoiding everyone, and roamed the ravaged ship, seeking a place of privacy. He found it deep in the lower decks, near a boiler room, behind a pile of timbers that had been used to shore up a rupture in the hull. He threw himself down on the oily deck, not caring about his white uniform, and cried for an hour — great, wracking sobs that made his stomach hurt. He cried for Mr. Scott, for Barney, for Lieutenant Goldberg, for all the men whose last glimpse

of life had been the fin of a shark. He wanted to stay there
forever, curled up in the fetal position, never again to
smell the stench of death, to fill little cloth sacks. Then
he felt a hand on his shoulder and looked up into the
eyes of a CPO in greasy dungarees — a stocky, older man
from the black gang.

"Get your ass topside, kid," he said gently. "You'll
feel better in the morning."

And Nick did. It was as though the memorial service
had been a turning point, a juncture; he could fall victim
to the horror of his experience, or, having cried it all out,
the grief, the self-pity, he could start looking to the future, to home and family — to Franny. There had been
no mail since they'd left Iwo, but Franny's old letters had
escaped the flames. He kept them under his mattress, in
a clean sock, and read a few of them every night, in the
light of the gooseneck lamp the shipfitter had installed.
The letters kept him going.

The memorial service had been a turning point for
Hildy, too, but in a different way. He became increasingly morose, withdrawn, even bitter at times. He spent
most of his time in the ready room or on the fifteen-foot
strip of undamaged catwalk adjacent to it, playing acey-
deucy or checkers with anyone who happened by — or
gin rummy. He seldom spoke of Diane or of the good
times at Quonset Point, and when scuttlebutt circulated
that Captain Rawlins had put him up for a major decora-
tion, he seemed uninterested. At first, Nick thought it
was simply frustration over his injuries. The swollen knee
was very painful, and when the bandage was removed
from his face, it was obvious that the gash would leave a
disfiguring scar. But his grim outlook seemed to go deeper
than that. He apparently had had second thoughts about

Princeton; Nick had found the application form, crumpled and discarded, in the ammo crate they were using as a trash receptacle. He seemed indifferent to everything, as though, having given so much of himself to others — through his leadership, his bouyant spirits, his superb abilities — he had run out of gas and had nothing left for coping with the changes that had come into his life. He brooded over Mr. Scott's death.

"If I'd just seen that Zeke sooner," he would say. "Even one second might've made a difference."

Not even the sinking of the *Yamato* moved him. They were now able to pick up the AFRS radio news reports from Hawaii. Enemy troops on Okinawa were digging in for a fight to the death; Tenth Army casualties were mounting rapidly. On April 6, the Japs launched a massive kamikaze attack on Task Force 58 — three hundred and fifty-five planes. The carriers escaped major damage, but the destroyers on radar picket duty were bloodied horribly. The *Newcomb* took five kamikaze hits; the *Aaron Ward,* seven. Later that day, the *Yamato,* as feared, sortied from the Inland Sea, screened by eight destroyers and one cruiser, and began a desperate run to Okinawa, to turn her big guns on American land forces and the ships that were supplying them. The submarines *Threadfin* and *Hackleback* tracked the flotilla through the China Sea. The next day, in an attack that lasted two hours and involved two hundred and eighty planes, Task Force 58's air groups sent the mighty battleship and her consorts to the bottom. Ten planes and twelve airmen were lost in the effort. Planes from the *Bennington* scored three hits.

"At least some of the Gumdrops were in on the kill," Nick said.

Hildy was unimpressed.

"It took nearly three hundred planes to do it," he said. "With better fighter cover, we could've done it with sixteen."

"But we didn't have the fighters."

"I know that," Hildy said irritably. "Jesus Christ, Nick, do you think I've got amnesia or something?"

"It wouldn't surprise me," Nick said. "You sure aren't the same guy who shot down the target sleeve."

Nick had wondered about Florence Snyder. Surely she had gotten the news by now; word of the wipe-out of VT-43 had spread throughout the Navy. They should send her a note, he thought — but after another AFRS report, it became unnecessary. The *Comfort* had been steaming fifty miles southeast of Okinawa, bound for Saipan with a load of wounded. One night, under a full moon, with the ship fully lighted and painted with a large red cross, in accordance with the internationally accepted precepts of the Geneva Convention, it was crashed by a kamikaze. The plane circled the ship carefully, then dived into the superstructure. Surgery was in progress. Everyone in the operating room was killed instantly — Miss Snyder, six other nurses, doctors, patients. Hildy switched off the radio.

"Those goddamn barbarians," he said. "They didn't even leave a girl to grieve over him."

He started out to the catwalk, stumbling on his crutches.

"I'll give you a hand," Nick said.

"Let me alone, Nick," he said tightly. "I'm okay."

Since it was difficult for Hildy to negotiate the ladders down to the ship's one operating mess compartment, on Three Deck, his friends in the galley inaugurated room service. Three times a day, a mess boy appeared at the ready room with a food carrier containing a hot meal. The same service was offered to Nick, who declined it, preferring the crowded, lively atmosphere of the general mess, which now featured a sign above the steam table: *The Only Cafeteria in Town.* The privileges of rank were suspended. Officers and enlisted men lined up together, first come, first served. The lowliest seaman was apt to find himself sitting across from the captain. The ship's stores had been fully replenished, but many of the ovens and ranges were beyond repair. The commissary officer had a standard retort for complainers.

"If you saw the galley," he would say, "you'd give us a medal for being able to boil water."

The mess also served as a social center for all hands, including the *Shiloh*'s eighty-six bed patients — a figure that explained Captain Rawlins's requisition of the canvas cots. Sick bay facilities had been improvised wherever undamaged space and electrical power were available — in machine shops, offices, even gear lockers. But after evening chow, at the captain's orders, bed patients were moved to cots in the mess compartment for recreation and entertainment.

"We've still got a few weeks before we reach New York," he said the night the new routine went into effect. "Maybe these get-togethers will help ease your pain and improve your morale."

The programs were varied. Twice a week, movies were shown — the films, projector, and screen courtesy of the *Ann Arbor.* There were games and sing-alongs, and on Sundays the bakers somehow managed to turn out enough cake for all hands, white cake, usually, with caramel frosting and a dollop of ice cream — the ice cream courtesy of the *Terre Haute.*

The first program featured a suspense film with Ingrid Bergman. Nick thought Hildy surely would want to see it.

"I don't think so, Nick," he said. "AFRS is broadcasting Woody Herman's band tonight."

"But you said yourself Bergman's the best actress in Hollywood."

"Don't push it, Nick," Hildy said. "I've got everything I need here in the ready room."

"Everything but Ingrid Bergman," Nick replied sarcastically. "And a good disposition."

Nick felt awkward, attending the social hours alone, but his resentment of Hildy faded in the congenial atmosphere of the gatherings. The less seriously wounded helped the doctors and corpsmen look after the men in the cots, fluffing pillows, running bedpans to the head, reading to them when there was a lull in the activities. Nick adopted a burn victim, a young plane handler swathed in bandages, like a mummy, and read short stories to him from *Collier's* and *The Saturday Evening Post* — the magazines courtesy of the destroyers. The boy's larynx had been scorched, and his voice was very weak. One night, noticing how difficult it was for Nick to hold a magazine in his left hand, he motioned for him to put his ear close.

"Too bad about your hand," he whispered.

When the *Shiloh* cleared the Panama Canal and was steaming north through the Caribbean, Hildy's radio was able to pick up broadcasts from the States. Every night, after taps, the two of them would lie in the ready room in the dark, smoking and listening to dance orchestras from the best hotels around the country — the Palmer House in Chicago, the Mark Hopkins in San Francisco, and one night, to Nick's great excitement, the Bellevue-

Stratford in Philadelphia. Remembering the prep school dances he'd attended at the Bellevue, the perfumed air, the rustle of organdy gowns, he tried to picture himself dancing with Franny — and couldn't. His stump would be an embarrassment, a crude appendage jabbing her ribs. Even with an artificial hand, it wouldn't be any good. You couldn't twirl a girl with a wooden hand, or stroke her hair, or — do other things. And he began to have deep misgivings about his homecoming. It was too soon, from kamikazes to perfumed air in just one month. He needed time. The ship was scheduled to dock at the Brooklyn Navy Yard on April 19, in the afternoon. He hoped something would happen to delay them, so that it would be dark when they arrived. By daylight, onlookers would see the disreputable condition of the ship and its crew and think they'd made a mess of things.

On the *Shiloh*'s last night at sea, the social hour featured a talent show, for which the participants had spent a week rehearsing. Captain Rawlins, who had a deep, rich voice, had volunteered to form a barbershop quartet and picked Nick to be first tenor. Nick was proud that the captain had chosen him.

It was a good evening. The long ordeal was almost over. The bakers surprised everyone with devil's food cake, and the *Terre Haute* sent over a double ration of ice cream, along with a good luck message signed by every member of her crew. The *Shiloh* was steaming in rough seas, off Cape Hatteras, North Carolina, and the pitching of the deck added to the hilarity of some of the acts. There were several excellent comedy routines, and a soft-shoe chorus line of boatswain's mates, who imitated musical instruments as they danced. The chaplain gave a dramatic reading of a Rudyard Kipling poem, and a seventeen-year-old yeoman, a shy boy from Poplar Bluff, Missouri, sang "Stardust" in a voice clear as a bell. The quartet was last, introduced by the disbursing officer: "And now, direct from Kamikaze Arms in the beautiful China Sea, the Shiloh-Tones, featuring that idol of the airwaves, Iron Gut Rawlins!"

The quartet did "Ida," "Sweet Georgia Brown," and "Carolina Moon." Their finale, a ribald barracks ballad, brought down the house.

> Oh, she jumped in bed and covered up her head
> And said I couldn't find her,
> But I knew damn well she was lyin' like hell,
> 'Cause I jumped right in behind her!

The crowd went wild. Captain Rawlins, smiling with pleasure, bowed deeply, then came to attention and saluted his men.

"You're a great bunch," he bellowed above the noise. "If the Japs hadn't smashed up our restoratives, I'd stand drinks for the house."

And as the men clapped and cheered, Nick knew it was a night they would all remember — the men with no eyes, the amputees, the burn cases wrapped like mummies. A bond had formed between them that would last forever.

They were the men of the *Shiloh.* They had kept their ship afloat to fight another day.

PART THREE: THE HOSPITAL

14. JUST FOUR MONTHS

THE VAST NAVY YARD WAS A DIN OF ACTIV-
ity. Pneumatic hammers clattered everywhere, and powerful cranes moved huge gun barrels and steel plates
against the darkening sky. Nick and Hildy, their seabags
packed, watched from an undamaged section of the starboard catwalk as tugboats nudged the *Shiloh* to its moor-
ing, where workmen in metal hats were already stringing
cables and erecting scaffolding in order to start repairs on
the battered carrier.

"I hate to see her end up here," Hildy said.

"It beats the bottom of the China Sea," Nick said.
"Consider it a hospital. She'll be a hundred percent when
they've finished with her."

"I stuck a hunk of shrapnel in my seabag," Hildy
said. "For a souvenir."

"So did I," Nick said. "A piece of the ready room."

"She's a great ship," Hildy said. "I'll never forget
her."

It took several hours to remove the wounded from
the *Shiloh* and load them into the ambulances and buses
that were lined up on the dock. Bed patients, each lying
flat in a wire basket, were lowered to the dock one by one
by a winch. Hildy left the ship via wire basket; Nick was

allowed to use the gangway, escorted by a corpsman. It was dark when their bus finally pulled away from the *Shiloh,* a white hospital bus marked with red crosses, with Nick and Hildy wrapped in blankets and strapped into canvas stretchers. Nick thought that the stretchers were carrying things a bit far; he and Hildy were listed as ambulatory patients.

"Regulations," the corpsman said. "It's just till we get to the hospital."

But he loosened Nick's straps so that he could lean on an elbow and look out the window. It was a misty April evening. The bus turned out of the Navy Yard and into a commercial thoroughfare. Nick noticed little things — street lights, a stray dog, three men arguing in front of a tavern, a Coca-Cola sign in a drug store window. So normal, he thought, yet so unreal, and he felt oddly out of place. At a stoplight, he could make out the headlines at a corner newsstand. The fighting was still raging in Okinawa. In Europe, Russian armies were closing in on Berlin. President Truman had addressed Congress. Truman. Nick couldn't get used to the name. They had been nearing the Panama Canal, a week ago, when news of President Roosevelt's death was radioed to the *Shiloh.* Nick had never heard of Truman. So many complications, he thought. A new President. Mr. Scott dead. A stump where his right hand used to be. Hildy's bad knee and growing bitterness. His first meeting with Franny and with his parents, both of which he dreaded. He felt dirty and tainted and wasn't ready to meet anyone. Luckily, there would be time. At Ulithi, there'd been a mail pickup. He had sent letters to Franny and to his father — in Doc Boyd's handwriting — cheerful, reassuring letters that alluded to a superficial injury to his right hand. Yes, there would be time. Franny would be at Wickford until late in May. Perhaps he could even put it off until he'd been fitted with an artificial hand —

The hospital was in a congested district of Brooklyn, on the waterfront, sheltered from the clamor of passing traffic by a brick wall overgrown with ivy. The bus went through a paved courtyard and around to a portico in the North Wing. Hospital personnel were hurrying out to receive them — doctors, corpsmen, Red Cross volunteers, Navy nurses with insignias of gold and blue in their white caps. Seeing them, Nick had the same feeling he'd had when Task Force 58 rallied around the *Shiloh* — the Navy taking care of its own.

"Hildebrandt, Philip L.," a voice called out as they stepped off the bus. "Enright, Nicholas J."

"Here, sir," Nick responded.

A doctor wearing a long white coat over his khaki uniform came forward. He was a short, swarthy man, about forty, who smelled of ether and tobacco.

"Get their records, Pinkie," he said, snapping his fingers at a red-haired corpsman, and to Nick and Hildy, "I'm Lieutenant Commander D'Amato. For better or for worse, you are now my patients. Let's hope it will be a mutually rewarding relationship."

The corpsman brought their medical records.

"As you can see, we're very crowded," Dr. D'Amato said, scanning the folders. "Saipan, Iwo, Okinawa — there's no end to it. We're putting you in the Penthouse, but don't feel grateful. It's a glorified mop closet that we can squeeze six beds into. But it's better than a corridor."

He gave Nick a brisk once-over.

"Is that stump your only problem, Enright?"

"As far as I know, sir."

"Well, we'll soon find out. Hildebrandt, you're a mess. That's an ugly scar, but we can pretty it up a bit. Let's take a look at that knee."

The corpsman brought a wheelchair. Hildy handed his crutches to Nick and sat down, his stiff left leg extended. The corpsman undid the safety pins where the trouser leg had been slit.

"You've got a problem, son." The doctor poked and squeezed the swollen knee; Hildy flinched from the pain. "I want you to stay off that leg. We'll get some X rays in the morning, but meantime don't so much as touch a toe to the deck. You can go to the head, on crutches, but that's all. Understand, Phil?"

"Everyone calls him Hildy, sir," Nick said. "I'm Nick."

"I take it the two of you are friends?"

"Yes, sir," Nick replied, irked at Hildy's silence; normally, he handled such matters. "We were crewmen on the same TBF."

"Oh?" The doctor looked at them with new interest. "The *Shiloh*'s air group?"

"Yes, sir. VT-43."

"Yes, the torpedo squadron." He nodded his head slowly. "Then you — you're the survivors?"

"Yes, sir."

He glanced from Nick to Hildy without saying anything. There was a great tiredness in his eyes, Nick thought. Then he smiled and extended a hand. "God bless you both," he said. "It's a privilege to be your physician."

He turned and started over to two stretcher cases.

"Pinkie, only two beds in the Penthouse, you hear? And see that these men get anything they want." He looked back at Nick and winked. "Within reason, of course."

And then ensued what Nick would remember as "the Big Sleep." From Thursday night till Saturday afternoon, he and Hildy did nothing but sleep, deeply, luxuriantly, waking only for meals and for trips to the head. Dr. D'Amato was there when Nick woke for lunch Saturday, and checked the dressing on his stump.

"I don't understand it," Nick said apologetically, and yawned. "All we did our last month at sea was loaf."

"It's a delayed reaction," Dr. D'Amato said, amused. "Your medical problems will wait. Go back to sleep."

Nick was already dozing off again, thinking how safe the hospital was, how quiet. No rumbling of turbines, no sharks, no kamikazes, no GQ gong jarring you out of your bunk in a cold sweat. Just clean sheets and cool, fresh milk, so rich it left a mustache when you drank it. God, he couldn't get enough of it! He would have to talk to Franny about it. "Franny, you've got to keep plenty of milk in the icebox." And then he was drifting in a lovely montage of dreams. Franny at the Point. Franny on a beach somewhere, in a bathing suit with a little skirt that bounced when she ran through the surf. He and Franny in front of the fireplace at the Biltmore, the glow of the embers flickering in her eyes, those quick, almond eyes, coming closer and closer, and her lips, cool at first, then warm and moist —

"There. I've kissed you awake. Just like the fairy prince."

He saw her in a blur at first, leaning over the bed, smiling, in a white blouse and a pale blue skirt, her dark hair done in a new way, pulled back in a bun — and it was as if they'd never been apart.

"Franny!" He sat up in the bed, keeping his right arm under the covers. "How long have you been here?"

"Since yesterday, off and on." Her eyes glowed with happiness. "I kept missing you when you were awake."

"But why didn't you have them wake me?"

"I wanted to surprise you. Besides, you look so blissful when you're sleeping."

"Have you seen Hildy?" Nick looked over at his bed; it was empty.

"They said he's down in X ray."

Nick started to laugh.

"What's so funny?"

"Us," he said. "Our big moments are always so undramatic. Remember the night we decided to be married? We sort of ease into things."

"We don't need dramatics, Nickie," she said. "We're sure of each other."

"But I don't understand, Franny. How on earth did you know when we'd be docking? Or where?"

"Silly boy. The *Shiloh*'s been all over the front pages. President Roosevelt issued a citation before he died. He said no ship in the history of the Navy ever took such a beating and stayed afloat. You're all heroes."

"Not really," Nick said. "Just afraid of sharks."

"Then my compliments to the sharks." She sat down on the bed and ran her fingers through his tousled hair. "There was a bulletin on the radio when the *Shiloh* steamed into the harbor. I was so excited. All I could think of was 'He's back. He's back.' "

"Actually, Franny, not all of me is back."

Their eyes met and held.

"Yes," she said quietly. "I know."

"You do?"

"Dr. D'Amato told me. But I'd known before that. I called your father. We were both suspicious about your letters. He talked to a friend in the Navy Department."

"Then — it's all right?"

"Of course, silly." She stroked the outline of his right arm. "Is it painful?"

"Just a dull ache." Nick pulled the bandaged arm from under the covers and waved it about like a wand. "The bandage is mainly for protection. It's pretty well healed, but they'll probably have to trim off a little more. Doc Boyd was sort of rushed when he patched it up."

"What about Hildy's leg?"

"It's his knee," Nick said. "And his face was cut up pretty badly."

As they talked, Nick found that he could discuss the *Shiloh* only in general terms, as though reporting on a highway accident or the effects of a thunderstorm. He told her about Mr. Scott, but not of his slow bleeding to death, or the hasty jettisoning of Raspberry One into the sea with his body still in it. He told her of his hand being severed by flying shrapnel, but not of the carnage on the flight deck, nor the blood gushing in the scuppers, nor of the great explosions that splattered human entrails in his face. In the surroundings of the hospital, with its ivy-covered wall and abundance of milk; in the presence of Franny, with her white blouse and blue skirt, her fresh face and clear eyes — the grisly realities of war seemed a contamination. However, he told her about Hildy's heroism — sketchily.

"Hildy." Franny sighed deeply, as though sensing the details Nick had withheld. "Equal to any occasion."

"He's not equal to this one, I'm afraid," Nick said.

"They're not going to amputate or anything? —"

"It's not his injuries," Nick said. "It's — I don't know. Everything hit him at once. He's not the same old Hildy. I'm worried."

Franny sat down on the bed and rested her chin in her hand. "Damn!" she said. "I wish Diane had come with me."

"So do I," Nick said. "Hildy could — "

They were interrupted by a commotion out in the corridor, followed by Hildy's angry voice.

"You clumsy pecker-checker! Watch where you're steering this damn thing!"

And then Hildy rolled into the Penthouse, in a wheelchair pushed by Pinkie, the corpsman. His mouth fell open when he saw Franny.

"I don't believe it," he said, wide-eyed.

For a second, Franny's eyes betrayed the anguish she felt at seeing the changes in Hildy — the stiff leg, now in a metal splint, the hardened eyes, the long, disfiguring purple welt that ran down the left side of his face, distorting his smile. Then the moment was gone, and she ran to the end of the room to greet him.

"Hildy, Hildy, Hildy!" She smiled happily and threw her arms around him. "Oh, it's so good to see you!"

"Didn't Diane come with you?" he asked her, looking around the room.

"She couldn't," Franny said. "She's been campused."

Hildy was obviously disappointed — and hurt.

"They catch her smoking again?"

"Uh-huh," Franny said. "In the library."

He managed a smile. "Leave it to Diane," he said. "Hey, this calls for a party. Pinkie, three coffees."

They spent the remainder of Franny's visit gathered around Nick's bed, talking — Nick and Hildy in hospital pajamas and white terrycloth robes with blue *USN* monograms. Franny said she couldn't get used to the sight of Hildy smoking a cigarette. Hildy said he couldn't get used to the sight of Franny without knee socks. "I think I've outgrown them," she said, and they all laughed. Hildy wanted to know all about Rhode Island. Quonset Point wasn't the same, Franny told them. All of the air groups had gone, to West Coast air bases, and she'd heard that two of the barracks had been boarded up. There was talk that the casino might not reopen next year; with the war in Europe drawing to a close, the factories had cut back, and business was down. She and Diane had stopped by their spot at the Biltmore one night, but hardly anyone was there, and they decided not to stay.

"It's hard to imagine the old place without people three-deep at the bar," Hildy said.

They talked about the Point and the casino and the party they'd crashed at the Knickerbocker, at which Diane had gotten sick on rum and Coke.

"She was white as a sheet," Nick recalled, laughing. "Hildy practically had to carry her to the train."

Franny smiled wistfully. "They were good times, weren't they?" she said.

And for a moment, her composure cracked.

"It seems so long ago," she said, her eyes filling with tears. "But it's been just four months . . ."

15. In Trust

NICK AND HILDY HAD EXPECTED A RELA-tively short stay at the hospital; a month, perhaps six weeks. Nick knew it was the end of the line for him; the Navy had no place for one-handed aircrewmen. But Hildy assumed he would be returned to active duty when his knee healed — to one of the new air groups that were being formed, at Norfolk and at San Diego, in preparation for the invasion of Japan. Dr. D'Amato, however, had a different prognosis.

"You're going to have to face it, Hildy," he said when he showed him the X rays of his bad knee. "You're never going to regain full use of that leg. Seventy percent, if the surgery goes well; eighty percent at best. Right now, I'd settle for fifty percent."

Hildy was stunned.

"But it doesn't seem that serious, Doc," he said. "Just a little swelling."

"Count your blessings, son," Dr. D'Amato said gently. "It could've been worse."

"I don't consider a bum leg much of a blessing," Hildy said resentfully.

"Maybe not," Dr. D'Amato said, "but it beats a white cross. My friends in Intelligence say the invasion of Japan is going to make Okinawa look like a skirmish. You'll be a lot safer back in Minnesota."

Hildy was unmoved by the doctor's logic. In a way, Nick shared his disappointment. They were out of the war, through no fault of their own, and would miss — or be spared — the culmination of the long Pacific campaign. His feelings were mixed. Gratitude, yes, but a nagging sense of guilt, too. Had they been given an easy way out?

"What about my scar?" Hildy said.

"You won't recognize yourself," Dr. D'Amato said. "There'll still be some slight disfiguration at the corner of your mouth, but it can't be helped. Muscle damage."

Because of the heavy backlog of *Shiloh* surgical cases, Hildy wasn't operated on until May 7, which was the day the Germans surrendered, thus ending the war in Europe. Dr. D'Amato estimated that the surgery, which was very delicate, would take two to three hours. It took four. Nick spent the time making his first tour of the hospital and its grounds, in pajamas and robe, acquainting himself with his new surroundings — the Ship's Service store, where he bought two Milky Ways and an ice cream cone; the library, which had a fine selection of books and magazines; the solarium, a recreation lounge for patients, where movies were shown three nights a week. It was a long, airy room, with French windows that opened on a veranda bordered by juniper shrubs and a box hedge. Below the veranda, the West Lawn sloped down to the waterfront, Upper New York Bay, where there was a view of Ellis Island, the Statue of Liberty, and, across the bay, the New Jersey skyline. It was very pleasant, Nick thought. Dr. D'Amato had told him that his own surgery, the amputation of a few more inches of his arm to provide a smooth surface for an artificial device, wasn't scheduled for another week. It would be soon enough; he was in no hurry.

"Hey, buddy," a patient in a wheelchair called to him, "you one of the new guys in the Penthouse?"

"Yes," Nick answered, and introduced himself. "Nick Enright, Philadelphia."

"Mike Grabowski, Toledo." The boy, who had no legs, was wearing a Marine fatigue cap, set at a jaunty angle. "Where'd you lose that hand, Nick?"

"The *Shiloh*."

"I was at Iwo." The boy slapped his two stumps. "Fourth Marines. Were you ship's company?"

"No," Nick said. "Air group. I was a crewman on a TBF."

"No bull?" the boy asked, and grinned. "A TBF

saved our ass. A Jap pillbox was wiping out the whole damn platoon, then a TBF made a run on it. Wham! No pillbox. Maybe it was you."

"Could be," Nick said. "We flew a lot of ground support over Iwo."

"Hey, drop by Ward B sometime," the boy said. "I took a samurai sword off a dead Jap colonel on Mount Suribachi. I'll show it to you."

"Sure," Nick said. "Maybe tomorrow."

In the library, which was adjacent to the main lobby, Nick ran across a copy of a Willa Cather novel that Franny had recommended and checked out a new Perry Mason for Hildy, who was fond of mysteries. Perhaps because of Dr. D'Amato's remarks, his eye fell on a selection of war journals in the periodical rack, one of which featured an analysis of the planned invasion of Japan. He thumbed through several of the journals, most of them quarterlies. The articles and commentaries, by historians and political scientists, seemed to give coherence to the vast global conflict of which he had been a part, but about which he knew virtually nothing. He checked out a stack of back issues, beginning with the German invasion of Poland in 1939, which had started it all, and took them up to the Penthouse. He still found it difficult to hold a book or a magazine in one hand, so he sat crosslegged on the bed, with the journals spread out on a pillow. The pages, however, kept leafing over. Pinkie, the corpsman, saw his problem.

"You need something to weigh them down," he said, and brought Nick an empty coffee mug.

"Thanks, Pinkie," Nick said.

Pinkie hung around at the foot of the bed. "There's scuttlebutt that Hildy's up for the Navy Cross," he said.

"Do tell," Nick said, wishing he'd go away.

"Geez, you guys must've had a hot time out there," Pinkie kept on. "You know, going after that Jap battleship and all — "

Nick ignored him. He didn't like Pinkie, who had a pasty complexion and pimples and was always eavesdropping. But more than that, he was discovering that he had no interest in men who hadn't seen combat. He felt uncomfortable in their presence and found their conversation irrelevant. Dr. D'Amato was an exception; he seemed to experience combat through the wounds he treated, sharing the pain, sensing the horror. But otherwise, Nick preferred the company of his *Shiloh* shipmates, who had come to regard the sole survivors of the torpedo squadron as mascots, symbols of the ship's great days. Those who could hobble around on crutches dropped by the Penthouse regularly, and Nick found the camaraderie deeply satisfying.

"You making it okay, Nick?" they would ask cheerfully; or, "Hildy, how's your goddamn knee?"

And they would sit and chat for a while. About simple things — the good taste of fresh orange juice, the fun of seeing a Mickey Mouse cartoon again, the sweet behind of one of the Red Cross volunteers. They seldom mentioned the ordeal they'd shared; it was enough just to be together. But Nick knew that in the privacy of their souls, they all searched for an answer to the unanswerable. *Why was I spared?* And it seemed to him that they, the survivors, held the lives of their dead shipmates in trust, would always hold them in trust, and that one day there would be an accounting.

"You know something, Nick?" Hildy said the night they were served their first steak dinner — Nick's meat having been cut for him. "The whole squadron, planes and all, is on the other side of the world, at the bottom of some damn ocean, and here we are in a mop closet in Brooklyn, eating steak and mushrooms. It makes you think, doesn't it?"

Steak was on the menu again when Hildy came out of surgery, but he was in severe pain and sick from the anesthesia, ether, and couldn't eat. His entire left leg was encased in a heavy cast, bent slightly at the knee, which he would be required to wear for eleven weeks. Dr. D'Amato, in operating room garb, came by the Penthouse while Hildy was still out.

"He's in for a rough time," he said to Nick. "When the cast comes off, he'll have to learn to walk all over again. If the surgery was a success, that is. The ligaments were a mess."

"Is there anything I can do to help him?" Nick asked.

"Try to keep him from toppling over," Dr. D'Amato said. "The cast weighs a ton. Even crutches will be difficult for him."

That was the day Lieutenant Stritch came into their lives — a large, mature woman, who before Pearl Harbor had been head nurse at a hospital in Vermont. She was in the Penthouse hourly, taking Hildy's pulse, checking his blood pressure, and when he came out of the anesthesia, she wasted no time in getting him to his feet.

"Off your backside, matey," she said in her flat New England accent. "We don't want your lungs filling up with fluid. You might come down with a case of pneumonia."

Hildy was in a foul mood.

"Let me alone," he said petulantly, and pushed her arm away. "Can't you see I'm sick?"

"Well, if you aren't the baby." Miss Stritch stood back with her hands on her hips. "I understand you shot down a dozen Jap Zeroes. How'd you do it, by throwing your diapers at them?"

Hildy gave her a fierce look and, with great effort, swung his heavy left leg out over the floor. "Hand me those crutches," he said to Miss Stritch. "And is there some way I can scratch inside the cast? The itching is driving me crazy."

"I came prepared," she replied, and produced a coat hanger, which she straightened and poked down the inside of the cast, from the thigh. "Tell me where."

"To the left," he said. "Now a little farther down. Ahh, right there."

A week later, Miss Stritch was getting Nick to his feet, his right arm heavily bandaged and in a sling, his stomach queasy, his stump throbbing painfully.

"How long will it take to heal?" he asked her.

"A month," she said. "Maybe six weeks. It should heal hard and smooth by the end of June. You'll be sent to Bethesda then, the big Naval hospital outside Washington. They've got a special prosthetics unit. We just get you ready."

It was a difficult week for Nick. Hildy was a poor companion, withdrawn, almost sullen, frustrated by his immobility and embarrassed by the necessity of having to be bathed by Miss Stritch. Despite his pain, however, he practiced stubbornly on the crutches, clomping noisily around the Penthouse, cursing bitterly when he stumbled.

"There's got to be an easier way, Nick," he said wearily one day. "The kamikazes are beginning to seem like the good old days."

Nights were the worst. Hildy was having bad dreams.

Nick would hear him tossing and groaning and wonder what he was dreaming about. The *Yamato?* The kids he'd splattered at Chichi Jima? Nick had had no problems with dreams, but he felt a growing depression. From his bed, through a west window, he could see the Jersey skyline. Now that the fear of enemy bombers was over, and people were no longer heeding the blackout regulations, the electric signs had been lit up again. The one that dominated the view was GAS IS BEST, with CLEAN, EFFICIENT, ECONOMICAL coming on in sequence. And he would stare, unseeing, at the blinking sign, sleepless from pain, brooding over the fate of mankind. The war journals he was reading gave a numbing scope to the war. Dunkirk, Tobruk, and Anzio; Stalingrad, Corregidor, and Tarawa. Battles he'd read about as an adolescent; and soon, the biggest one of all — the invasion of Japan. The journals projected a million American casualties, three to four million for the Japanese. Nick couldn't comprehend a million casualties. There weren't enough cemeteries to bury the dead, hospitals to treat the wounded.

He had paid a visit to Ward B to see the Toledo Marine's Samurai sword, unaware that the ward was reserved for the hospital's worst cases — men whose faces had been horribly disfigured, men with no arms, with no legs, with neither, basket cases who would spend the rest of their lives in veterans' hospitals. The Marine had already been transferred to Bethesda, but Nick had met Mrs. Sweeney, a civilian, a tiny, energetic woman who was in charge of the ward's Red Cross volunteers.

"It jolts you at first," she said, arranging an assortment of doughnuts on a food cart. "But in every one of those maimed bodies is a human soul."

Nick was badly shaken. He'd seen enough raw, man-gling injuries on the *Shiloh,* but somehow the aftermath was more disturbing.

"It's snack time," Mrs. Sweeney said. "Perhaps you wouldn't mind pushing the cart with your good hand while I help the girls serve."

Some of the patients were being hand-fed, like infants in a high chair. Nick, feeling like a gawker at a zoo, tried not to stare.

"I think this young man is trying to say something to you," Mrs. Sweeney said, pausing at the bed of a burn case who had no face. "What is it, Jimmy?"

"How's the boy, Nick?"

Nick looked at the boy's face and felt a moment's revulsion. There was something familiar about the voice, which was barely a whisper. The plane handler he'd adopted on the voyage home.

"Hey, buddy." He moved close to the bed and forced a smile. "What happened to your turban?"

"They're shipping me to Bethesda tomorrow," the boy whispered. "Skin grafts."

"I'm going to end up there too," Nick said. "I'll read you some of those *Tugboat Annie* stories."

"Swell, Nick."

The volunteer who had been feeding the boy raised a mug to his mouth.

"Finish your coffee, Jimmy," she said.

The mug had a glass straw in it. Afterward, that's what stayed in Nick's mind — hot coffee through a glass straw.

Mrs. Sweeney walked back with Nick to the Penthouse, which was how she discovered what Miss Stritch and Dr. D'Amato already knew — that it was a convenient place in which to take a break from their routines —

to relax and drink coffee and exchange scuttlebutt, with
Pinkie stationed out at the desk to alert them of any
emergency. When the three of them were there together,
the conversation was frequently hilarious. Dr. D'Amato,
who was using humor as therapy on Hildy, was full of
corny routines.

"You're from the farm belt, Hildy," he would say.
"Tell me, what do you think of cabbage as a head?" Or,
"As a visitor to New York, what do you think of the sub-
way as a hole?"

One day he tried a routine that Hildy was on to.
"Hildy, did you take a shower today?" he asked him, and
Mrs. Sweeney broke up when Hildy quickly retorted,
"Why? Is one missing?"

Mrs. Sweeney, a widow, ran a settlement house in a
tenement district of lower Manhattan, a neighborhood
center for handicapped children. She had relatives in
Germantown and enjoyed chatting with Nick about Philadelphia. And slowly, in the warmth of her company,
Nick's dark mood lifted, and he began to look to the future with increasing confidence. He made a mental list
of things he wanted to discuss with Franny when she
visited again — college, finances, the situation with her
father, a wedding date. He knew Hildy wasn't going to
apply to Princeton. Truthfully, he was having doubts
about Princeton himself. Six months ago, he had looked
forward to becoming a part of the school's venerable un-
dergraduate traditions, but now they seemed silly. He
would be a married student, he hoped; a disabled veteran
trying to make up for lost time. There would be no room
in his life for beer steins and fraternity paddles. Besides,
his ideas were changing. He had always expected to follow in his father's footsteps, in law, but now he wasn't

sure. He needed time to find himself academically. More than anything, he wanted to understand the experience he'd been through and then somehow work to ensure that his son, his and Franny's, would never march off to war. No, Princeton was out; Columbia would be more realistic, an urban campus that offered housing and employment possibilities. He would have the GI Bill and a small disability pension, but it might not be enough. It was important to him that he make it on his own, without accepting a penny from his father. Perhaps Franny could be persuaded to transfer to Barnard, the girls' college across the street from Columbia, for her remaining two years. They would find a basement apartment near the campus and shut out the war. There would be books everywhere, and at night, Franny would sit at a mirror, in her slip, brushing her smooth dark hair. Franny. God, he couldn't wait to see her again —

He saw her sooner than he'd expected, on the Wednesday before finals at Wickford, breezing into the Penthouse in a blue seersucker dress with a little white jacket, her arms loaded with supplies — a fountain pen and a bottle of ink, writing pads, pencils, her penmanship manuals from grade school, and a box of Milky Ways.

"One of the profs died," she said, out of breath, "and they canceled classes today. I've got to take a train back at six."

Miss Stritch was about to wheel Hildy out to the West Lawn for some sun.

"Where's Diane?" he asked Franny.

"She couldn't come."

"Campused?" he said. "Or squeamish?"

"It's not that, Hildy," Franny said, stooping to pick up an eraser. "She had to — "

"Never mind." He turned his head to hide his disappointment. "Let's go, Stritchie."

When they'd gone, Nick reached for the Milky Ways.

"Can't you stay overnight?" he said.

"I'd get demerits," Franny replied, dumping the articles on his bed. "How did the surgery go?"

"Okay. They removed the bandage yesterday."

"I knew it would be all right." She smiled and patted his right sleeve, which had been pinned up over his stump. "My father says Dr. D'Amato is a very good surgeon. Honestly, Nickie, don't you ever take off that robe?"

"You sound like my mother," he said. "What's all the junk?"

"You've got to learn to write with your left hand." She arranged the pencils and pads on the nightstand. "And not just the usual southpaw scrawl. Good penmanship."

"What's with Diane?"

"I'll tell you later," Franny said. "Now get busy."

She kept him at work for two hours, urging him to use his wrist, not his fingers — page after page of exercises from the manuals, ovals and slanted lines, then the first few letters of the alphabet, both capitals and lower case.

"Guess what," she said as he worked. "I'm transferring to Barnard."

Nick looked up at her and laughed. "Franny," he said, "you amaze me. I was going to suggest Barnard to you. I've decided on Columbia."

"I figured you would. That's why I'm transferring."

"But how could you be so sure?"

"It's the practical thing to do," she said. "Besides,

you're not Princeton. Not anymore. It's a snob school."

"So is Wickford. Not that I'm complaining, but how did you end up there, anyway?"

"It's a good school," she said. "They've got the best lit department in the East. Oh, I know what you're thinking — anti-Semitism, quotas for Jews, that sort of thing. But that's true of a lot of schools."

"Has it been much of a problem at Wickford?"

"Not really. Of course, Diane has been an advantage. It's hard to snub Betty Coed's roommate. There are a few snotty girls who look down their noses at me. But that doesn't bother me; I look down my nose at them. The ones that gall me are the phony liberals."

"I know the type," Nick said. "Don't-get-me-wrong-some-of-my-best-friends-are-Jewish."

"Or Catholic."

"Touché."

They both laughed.

"I suppose you've got our wedding date all figured out, too."

"Uh-huh. December twenty-fourth."

"December twenty-fourth? But that's Christmas Eve."

"Of course," Franny said. "That's why I chose it. Every December, I'll have Hanukkah, you'll have Christmas, and we'll both have our anniversary."

"Clever," Nick said, smiling.

"I thought so." She leaned over and kissed his cheek. "Oh, Nickie, I can't wait till we're married."

"You don't have to."

"I know. But we will. You will. You're a Philadelphia square. I'll probably be deflowered with great propriety."

"Don't count on it," Nick said, stroking her thigh.

"Oh, God, Nickie! Not here!"

"Then where?"

"Outside. I saw a spot down near the waterfront."

Later, as they strolled up a graveled path on the West Lawn, munching candy bars — Franny having met Miss Stritch and Mrs. Sweeney, and paid her respects to Hildy and Dr. D'Amato — she told Nick about Diane.

"She's been making excuses. I don't think she's able to handle all that's happened — Hildy's injuries, the hospital."

"What about when the semester's over?" Nick asked.

"She's already got an excuse for that. She'll be a counselor at that fine arts camp in the Poconos. They want her there early. I feel sorry for Hildy. Seeing Diane might give him a lift."

"I'm not sure," Nick said. "I don't think anything would give him a lift. Has she been dating other guys?"

"No," Franny replied. "That's the funny part. She hasn't had a date since the *Shiloh* sailed. All she does is paint. She's become obsessed with it."

"I can understand that — searching for a new direction. I'm sort of in the same boat." And he told her about the war journals and the influence they'd had on his thinking.

"Maybe those journals have already given you a direction," Franny said. "History. An academic career. You'd be very distinguished, actually. Professor Enright with the gloved hand. Which reminds me. Why have you got your sleeve pinned up? Are you ashamed of your stump?"

"I don't know," Nick said. "It feels funny uncovered. Like going around with your fly open."

"Well, I'm going to see it sooner or later." She unfastened the safety pins and rolled up the sleeve. "Very interesting," she said, examining the stump with great curiosity. "Of course, if you have to make a phone call, you'll need a pretty big dial."

Nick laughed so hard he choked on his candy bar.

When it was time for her to leave, Franny wanted to take the subway, but it was four blocks to the nearest station, and Nick insisted that she call a cab. They waited for the cab out in the courtyard, on a bench next to the flagpole, which was in the center of a bed of yellow marigolds.

"You know, sometimes I have deep thoughts, Nickie," Franny said. "And I can't help thinking that if it weren't for the war, we never would have met — and you'd still have a right hand."

"Not necessarily," Nick said. "If there'd been no war, I might've gotten killed in a car wreck after a drunken party at Princeton. Who can say?"

"Then it was worth it?"

"Yes, Franny. It was worth it."

And as the cab pulled away and she waved through the rear window, her nose slightly sunburned and a happy glow in her eyes, Nick knew that that was how he truly felt.

16. CHIFFON CAKE AND ICED TEA

STARTING IN LATE MAY, AFTER WICKFORD let out, Franny came to the hospital nearly every day. Dr. D'Amato arranged for a special pass that allowed her to come and go as she pleased, using the fire staircase, which was just outside the Penthouse. Nick overheard him talking to Miss Stritch.

"There'll be no problem," he said. "They're off in the Penthouse by themselves, with nothing to do but wait for their limbs to heal. They're orphans, really. Their squadron was wiped out, and they'll be discharged as soon as we get them patched up. So we'll just try to make their last weeks in the Navy as pleasant as possible."

Miss Stritch, who seemed to be developing a motherly attitude toward Hildy, agreed.

"I'll have Pinkie move a table and some chairs in there," she said. "And maybe an acey-deucy board and some playing cards. With his bad leg, Hildy can't be tramping up and down to the solarium."

"Make it checkers," Dr. D'Amato said. "I'm very good at checkers."

A few days after Franny's first visit, Nick had telephoned his father, asking him to abide by certain ground rules.

"Dad, I'd rather you and Mother didn't visit me while I'm at the hospital. I don't want her to see me while my stump is still healing."

"That's very considerate of you, Nick, but she's not squeamish."

"I know, Dad, but she'll be less upset after I get an artificial hand. I guess they'll send me to Bethesda for that, and then I'll be discharged. All right?"

"Whatever you say, Nick."

"Another thing — I'm bringing Franny with me when I come home."

"Fine, son. Everything here is as ready as it will ever be."

When Hildy was able to get around on crutches,

Nick phoned Mr. Scott's mother to pay his respects. She invited them to tea the following afternoon. Nick asked Franny to come along, in case Hildy should have a problem.

"If he starts toppling over," he said, "I might not be able to handle him with just one hand."

They took a cab to Brooklyn Heights, which was on the East River, across from the Wall Street district of Manhattan. The Scotts' house was in a long row of brownstones on Remsen Street. Nick was reminded of Rittenhouse Square, the churches, the tall shade trees, the little park overlooking the river.

"It's nice to see that you're both getting on well," Mrs. Scott said as she led them through the house to the sun porch. "I'm sorry Bob's father couldn't be here, but he's in Washington frequently these days. The War Production Board."

They sat on wicker chairs around a glass-topped table. A pleasant afternoon breeze came in the windows. Mrs. Scott served chiffon cake and iced tea and offered them cigarettes. A matronly woman with silver hair, she wanted to know everything. Nick told her about the strike on the *Yamato,* the heavy enemy flak, Mr. Scott's wounds.

"I assume there was a proper burial," she said.

"Not exactly," Nick said. "We crashed on the flight deck. Other planes were still coming in. They had to jettison Raspberry One with his body still in the cockpit."

Nick was afraid that the grim details of her son's burial would upset her, but they didn't.

"I understand," she said, nodding her head slowly. "It was fitting, in a way. He loved that plane." She turned to Franny. "Are you the girl who painted the insignia?"

"No, ma'am," Franny said. "It was my roommate, Diane Webb."

"He was so proud of that insignia," Mrs. Scott said. "He sent us a snapshot of it."

She brought out a photo album. There were pictures of Mr. Scott at Annapolis, at flight school in Pensacola, and several of him with Nick and Hildy, at Fort Lauderdale, at Quonset Point, aboard the *Shiloh*.

"Holy cow!" Hildy said. "I've never seen any of these pictures."

They chatted amiably for an hour. Mrs. Scott was curious about every aspect of her son's life aboard ship, where he slept, where he ate, what he did for recreation. Then she asked the inevitable question.

"Your attack on the Japanese battleship — was it worth it?"

Nick thought of the young Marine from Ward B, the one he'd talked to the day of Hildy's surgery.

"We had nothing to match the *Yamato*'s big guns," he said. "She could have caused thousands of casualties at Okinawa. Yes, ma'am. It was worth it."

At five o'clock, Franny phoned for a cab. Hildy jotted down his and Nick's home addresses and left them with Mrs. Scott. She seemed comforted by their visit.

"I'm so glad you came," she said at the door. "Bob always spoke very highly of the two of you."

"He was such a good man, Mrs. Scott," Hildy said, tears in his eyes. "I wish it'd been me instead of him."

On the drive back, Hildy sat moodily in a corner of the cab, staring out the window. At the hospital, Nick and Franny came around to help him. He started to get out, then changed his mind.

"You two go in," he said. "I'm going to do some shopping."

"But it's five-thirty," Nick said. "The stores close at six."

"They're open late tonight. I saw it in the paper." He closed the door and turned to the driver. "Take me to Macy's."

"Wait a minute!" Nick cried in protest. "I'll go with you. You might need help."

"I'll be fine, Nick," Hildy said, and the cab drove off.

Nick stood in the courtyard, scratching his head.

"Do you think he'll be all right?" Franny asked him.

"I don't know." Nick looked worried. "He's acting kind of funny."

It was after midnight when Hildy returned to the hospital. In a Shore Patrol wagon. Drunk, his hat gone, one crutch broken, and his cast badly damaged. Pinkie, who had night duty, rolled him into the Penthouse in a wheelchair, his head lolling and his eyes red and glazed.

"The SPs found him stumbling around outside the Shamrock Bar," Pinkie said to Nick, who had stayed up reading, waiting for some word of Hildy.

Hildy looked at Nick with a silly grin. "Nick, ol' boy —" he said, and passed out.

"Did you call Dr. D'Amato, Pinkie?" Nick asked.

"He's on liberty. But Lieutenant Stritch is on duty. I'll go get her."

It took the three of them to get Hildy into bed. His left trouser leg, which had been slit and pinned to accommodate the cast, was torn, and his jumper was a mess, wet and stained from spilled drinks. Miss Stritch clipped the pants away with a pair of scissors.

"The hotshot aircrewman ain't much of a hotshot now, is he?" Pinkie said with a laugh.

"Shut up, Pinkie," Miss Stritch said.

She examined the cast, which was cracked in several places.

"Pinkie, run down and get two rolls of tape," she said. "The widest we've got."

"Do you think he damaged the knee?" Nick asked her.

"We'll know in the morning." She spread a blanket over Hildy, who was sleeping like a baby, and shook her head sadly. "We see a lot of tragedies in this hospital, Nick. Patients who've been maimed or dismembered or incinerated. And do you know what hits me the hardest? They're just kids."

Nick lay sleepless most of the night. Miss Stritch had taped up Hildy's cast securely, but Nick was afraid he'd thrash about in his sleep and damage it further. Around three o'clock, as he was dozing off, he heard Hildy call to him.

"Will you give me a hand, Nick? I've got to go to the head."

Nick turned on the lamp on the nightstand and got his robe. He helped Hildy into the wheelchair and pushed him across the corridor to the head, where he was sick.

"You'll feel better in the morning," Nick said, patting his face with a damp towel.

"Is that a promise?"

"No. It's a threat."

They both laughed.

Hildy stumbled getting back into bed. Nick made a sling with his stump and good hand and, gingerly, helped him swing the heavy cast into the bed.

"Did I have any packages when the SPs brought me back?" Hildy asked him.

"No. You didn't even have a hat."

"I must've left them at that bar."

"The Shamrock?"

"Yeah. It's only a few blocks away."

"I'll go over there tomorrow and get them."

"Thanks," Hildy said. "I'll have Miss Stritch mail them for me. I got one of those indoor barometers for my folks and a Brooklyn Dodgers pennant for my sister."

Nick turned out the lamp and pulled up a chair. They lit cigarettes and talked for a while.

"So you actually made it to Macy's," Nick said.

"Sure. I went through the whole store. It's not as nice as Wanamaker's."

"What did you do then?"

"Rode around in a cab. You know something, Nick? New York looks dirty. It's not like it was before."

"I've noticed it too," Nick said.

"I didn't even get a kick out of the Empire State Building. Everything seems sour."

"You'll feel better when your leg's okay. You can start picking up your life, planning college."

"About college, Nick. I never sent that application to Princeton."

"I know. I saw it in the trash in the ready room. I've been having second thoughts about Princeton myself."

"It was nice of your dad to go to all that trouble, but — I don't know. I wrote to the University of Minnesota, but I'm not even sure I'll follow through on that. I'm all punched out, Nick."

"Has Chichi Jima been bothering you?"

"That's the funny thing. I haven't dreamed about it once. You know what I dream about, Nick? Not Chichi or the kamikazes or the guys being eaten by sharks. I keep seeing Diane's insignia going under when Raspberry One sank. Remember when she gave us that insignia?"

"At Franny's." Nick's cigarette made an orange glow in the darkness. "Dr. Kaplan proposed a toast."

"That was a sweet evening," Hildy said. "He said 'Godspeed,' and three months later we were in the middle of the China Sea with brains flying all over." He choked up. "I've lost my bearings, Nick. I thought I had everything figured out, but I've got to start all over — "

It pained Nick to watch helplessly as his friend struggled to find his way back. Only Dr. D'Amato, through his corny jokes, seemed able to kindle an occasional spark of the old Hildy. In the morning, sensing that Hildy was confused and depressed, the doctor went easy on him.

"I understand you took in a bit of the local color last night," he said while he examined the damaged cast.

"A little," Hildy said. "I don't think I could stand a lot."

"And what do you think of New York as a hole?"

Hildy managed a grin. "It's a fine place to live," he said, "but I'd hate to visit here."

"Well," Dr. D'Amato said, "we may be able to accommodate you. If you've screwed up the surgery, you'll be on a train to Great Lakes."

"Why Great Lakes?"

"Because the best orthopedic surgeon in the country happens to be on the staff of the Naval hospital there. I'm good, but he's developed a new technique for repairing ligaments."

He moved to the wall calendar, next to the utility sink, and took out his fountain pen.

"The cast can be repaired without disturbing the

knee," he said. "So here's what we'll do. It was due to come off on July twenty-third, but we'll keep it on for an extra two weeks, just to play safe." He circled August 4. "And you'd better stay out of the bars," he admonished Hildy, "or you'll still be here at Christmas."

After lunch, Nick walked over to the Shamrock Bar, which was in a residential section east of the hospital. He was immediately struck by the similarities to Red Wing — the tall elms that canopied the street, the large but unpretentious houses with wide lawns. In one yard, a little girl sat in a makeshift swing, an old tire suspended from the limb of a tree by a rope. It was a small-town neighborhood, and he wondered how Hildy had discovered it.

"I could've sworn I was walking up High Street in Red Wing," he told Franny when she visited that evening.

"Maybe he's just homesick," she said.

"Do you really think so?"

"No." She sighed. "Poor Hildy. I hate what's happening to him. He was the reason for everything, and I have a terrible fear that he's going to end up with a pension and a cane, hanging around some American Legion bar."

The next day, the big story in the papers was the founding conference of a new international organization, the United Nations, which was being held in San Francisco. On Okinawa, the First Marines had begun a final push to wipe out remaining Japanese resistance. American casualties so far numbered nearly fifty thousand: thirteen thousand killed and thirty-seven thousand wounded. The Navy alone listed five thousand dead and forty-eight hundred wounded. Nick wondered whether he and Hildy were included in those figures; the *Yamato* strike was in support of the Okinawa campaign. On the editorial page of the *Herald Tribune* there was a column speculating on how soon Okinawa would be available as a staging area for the invasion of Japan.

Well, at least he was out of it, he thought — and feelings of guilt gnawed at him again, about having been given an easy way out. When Franny visited, he asked her to write a letter for him, to Barney Jacob's widow.

"She lives in a little town in Illinois," he said. "I want to visit her after I'm discharged. I think it would help her to talk with someone from Barney's squadron."

"Am I going with you?"

"Naturally."

Nick felt better after Franny mailed the letter. It was a positive act.

17. LITTLE WARS

AS THE WEEKS WENT BY, IT OCCURRED TO Nick that the hospital was changing his life in unexpected ways. Soon it began to change Franny's, too.

One day, shortly before noon, Mrs. Sweeney, very agitated, appeared in the Penthouse and asked Franny whether she would fill in briefly for a girl who had an important errand to run. Nick wanted to warn Franny of what to expect in Ward B, but there was no opportunity.

"Meals are our busiest time," Mrs. Sweeney said as the two of them walked out into the corridor. "I'd ask a corpsman, but the feminine touch is so important to our patients."

They returned two hours later. Franny's face was white, her eyes fixed, and she smelled of bedpans. Nick thought she was going to faint.

"You've got a nice way with the patients, dear," Mrs. Sweeney said, putting an arm around her. "Perhaps you'd like to be one of our regulars. We could use an extra girl mornings. Six o'clock until lunch is over."

Nick knew that Franny had applied for a summer job at one of the New York publishing houses. He started to tell Mrs. Sweeney, but Franny cut him short.

"I'd be glad to, Mrs. Sweeney," she said. "I can't make it quite that early tomorrow, but the rest of the week is fine."

When Mrs. Sweeney had gone, Franny sat down on Nick's bed and gave a deep sigh. "Light me a cigarette, will you, Nickie?" she said.

"What about the Doubleday job?" Nick asked her, lighting a cigarette for each of them. "You were looking forward to it."

"After seeing Ward B," she said, "publishing seems frivolous."

"It's rough stuff. Do you think you can handle it?"

"You handled the *Shiloh*, didn't you? I'll talk to my father. He'll have some suggestions."

And so Franny became a Red Cross volunteer, in a gray uniform with red trim and a little nurse's cap, rising at five o'clock, arranging her father's breakfast, fixing cinnamon toast and coffee for herself, and then hurrying to the subway. On cool mornings, she threw a thin white sweater over her shoulders, cashmere with silver buttons, and if rain was forecast, she carried a colorful umbrella, of a red tartan design, that had belonged to her mother. She walked the four blocks from the subway station and was always the first volunteer to arrive.

"I don't know," Hildy said doubtfully. "Wickford girls aren't cut out for bedpans."

But there was more to her duties than bedpans and feedings; she read to the patients, wrote their letters, oftentimes just listened as they rambled on about home, family, girlfriends, the latter usually in past tense. Franny got to know them quite well.

"After a while, you don't notice their injuries," she told Nick. "You see the person inside. A few are bitter, but most of them are really nice boys. And they're so appreciative of the smallest thing you do for them, it makes me want to cry."

Soon Franny, too, was slipping away to the Penthouse occasionally, for coffee and a cigarette and to rest her feet, which were bothered by the floors. A marathon checkers match had evolved between Hildy and Dr. D'Amato, and when the doctor wasn't there, Franny played for him.

"We play for blood," Hildy warned her. "One false move, and Dr. D'Amato will cut out your appendix."

Franny worked three mornings a week — Mondays, Wednesdays, Fridays — and all day on Sundays, when most of the other girls attended church. On Sunday afternoons, she would gather flowers on the West Lawn, tea roses from the garden below the veranda, day lilies and foxglove from the perennial beds, which she arranged around the ward in vases she'd bought at Macy's basement. Nick carried the flowers in a straw basket and helped with the arrangements. Afterward, they would stroll down to the waterfront, where there was a seawall with a wrought-iron railing, and talk. Franny kept Nick filled in on her progress.

"I think Mrs. Sweeney is going to offer me a job at

her settlement house," she told him proudly. "It wouldn't pay much, but it'd be something I could work at part time after we're married, while I'm still going to school."

"You're really enjoying yourself, aren't you?" Nick said, pleased by her new interests.

"Yes, Nickie, I really am. I'm thinking of changing my major. Ward B isn't easy. I get tired and discouraged, but at the end of the day, I feel very good about myself."

That evening, after she got off duty, Franny stayed for the movie that was being shown in the solarium. It was a new Cary Grant film, a romantic comedy they both wanted to see, but they walked out, numb, following the newsreel, which showed hideous scenes of some of the liberated German concentration camps — Auschwitz, Treblinka, Belzec — where millions of prisoners, most of them Jews, had been put to death. The narration told a grim story of torture, starvation, slave labor. *"This, then, was the Third Reich's 'final solution' to what the Fuehrer called 'the Jewish problem.'"* There was footage of enormous gas chambers at Auschwitz. Two thousand victims would be herded in at one time — men, women, children, infants, screaming in terror, naked, their heads shaven — and when the doors were sealed, SS troopers dropped pellets of poison gas through a device in the roof. Other prisoners burned the corpses in big furnaces, and the smoke drifted out over the countryside.

"Let's get out of here," Nick whispered to Franny. "You're upset. I am, too."

"No," she said sharply. "I want to burn it into my mind. I never want to forget it."

A cartoon came on after the newsreel. Nick and Franny went out to the veranda. Nick noticed Dr. D'Amato in the back row, his head buried in his hands.

"How could they *do* it?" Franny was aghast. "A nation that has produced the most beautiful cantatas I've ever heard, exterminating my people like bugs."

She looked very vulnerable, Nick thought, like a hurt child, standing in the shadows near the juniper shrubs, in her gray uniform with its cute little cap. He didn't know what to say; the newsreel had said it all. He put an arm around her, hesitantly, his good one.

"They're my people, too, Franny," he said, knowing the words sounded empty. "They're everybody's people."

"No, they're not your people," she said, pulling away from him for a moment. "You could never understand —" Then she went into his arms and burst into tears. "I can't help it, Nickie," she said, sobbing. "All my father's friends in Heidelberg . . . all the cousins I've never seen . . . like bugs . . ." Nick let her cry. Then she blew her nose and wiped her eyes "I've got to go home," she said. "That newsreel is playing all over town. My father's probably seen it —"

Dr. Kaplan had seen the newsreel, and much more, but had been hiding it from Franny. With the enormity of the Nazi extermination scheme slowly coming into focus, government officials had invited members of his committee to view captured German films of the death camps. Some of the committee members had vomited; others had stared in disbelief as the scenes of horror unfolded — an actual execution, filmed through a concealed aperture in a gas chamber, and then the corpses being dragged from the chamber and trucked to the furnaces, which looked like ovens. Smiling Gestapo officers displayed lampshades made from the skins of young victims who had been especially executed for that purpose, a shot in the neck, usually, or a blow to the head, for the skin had to be free of defects in order to achieve an unblemished effect. The total number of murdered Jews was put at six million. Franny told Nick about it when she came in the next morning.

"I've never seen my father in such despair," she said. "I wanted to comfort him, but all I could think of was us. So I told him. After those films, what you and I have seemed good and clean and hopeful."

Nick had been waiting for her in the lobby. "How did he react?" he asked.

"He said he'd known all along. 'I'll not stand in your way, Franny,' he told me. 'The world has seen enough bitterness.' "

"I can't help feeling relieved," Nick remarked.

"Well, don't," she said. "We talked till midnight about some of the problems we're facing."

"Such as?"

"Not now, Nickie," she said. "I'm all problemed out. There's no point in brooding in advance. They'll be along soon enough."

They took the elevator up to the fourth floor.

"Are you sure you're up to working today?" Nick asked her.

"I'd fall apart without it," she replied. "Ward B is a great rock of sanity."

After breakfast, Nick played a few games of checkers with Hildy and then went down to the waterfront. He was confused over the events of last night. Although Franny had included him in her grief, she had instinctively pulled away from him, for only a moment, true; but it was enough to emphasize the fact that, in a very profound sense, they were strangers to each other. She could never share the warm feeling he got at Mass; he could never share an important part of her identity. He did not resent her for this; rather, he envied what was shut off from him. Jews were special, he was learning. They possessed a heritage, a continuity, an international bond of faith, which, if it could be achieved by other peoples, might bring peace and brotherhood. After all, who'd ever heard of Jews warring with each other? And as he was strolling along the seawall, thinking these things, a voice behind him said, "Six million Jews can't be wrong, huh, Nick?"

Nick turned around. It was Pinkie, grinning and pointing across the bay to where the outline of the unlighted GAS IS BEST sign showed on the Jersey skyline.

"I beg your pardon?" Nick said, puzzled.

"Six million Jews can't be wrong," Pinkie repeated, his grin turning into a smirk. "You know, them heebs in the German ovens."

Nick looked at Pinkie and then at the New Jersey shore — and something inside of him snapped.

"Why, you little son of a bitch," he muttered, and his right arm shot out like an arrow, before he remembered there was no fist attached to it.

"Hey!" Pinkie yelled, ducking. "What're you doing, for crying out loud!"

Nick's stump grazed Pinkie's head and smashed into the wrought-iron railing, but he caught him squarely in the jaw with a left, and then began flailing him with his stump, as though it were a whip. A rage welled up in him, a savagery, as it had that night on the *Shiloh* when he wanted to stalk the Japs and fight to the death; only now it was the Pinkies of the world that had to be stalked and wiped out — their sick jokes, their stupid smirks —

"Somebody help me, will you!" Pinkie screamed, shielding his face with his arms. "He's crazy!"

It took three corpsmen to pull Nick away. The pinned-up sleeve of his robe was wet with blood from his damaged stump. They took him to an emergency treatment room on the main floor. Both Dr. D'Amato and Miss Stritch had been called. Miss Stritch arrived first.

"Get that robe off," she ordered Nick. "It looks as if you've been mopping up strawberry soda with your sleeve."

She had the wound cleaned and a local anesthetic ready by the time Dr. D'Amato came in. Nick's wound had burst open under the impact of the iron railing.

"You pack a pretty mean stump, pardner," Dr. D'Amato said dryly, without humor. "They tell me you loosened four of Pinkie's front teeth. What did he do, trespass on your north forty?"

"Something like that," Nick said.

"Well, this will be good for another six weeks. You may never make it to Bethesda."

Nick's lacerations required extensive stitching, all of it intricate. When Dr. D'Amato had finished, Miss Stritch bandaged the stump, arranged the arm in a sling, and excused herself.

"I'll be in Pharmacy if you need me, Doctor," she said. "I've got medications to prepare."

Dr. D'Amato closed the door behind her and leaned back against an instrument cabinet, his arms folded.

"The CO wants a full report, Nick," he said. "What the hell got into you? Attacking hospital personnel. You could be court-martialed, amputee or no amputee."

"It was really nothing, sir. Just something Pinkie said."

"Like what?"

"I'd rather not say."

"I saw you and Franny at the movie last night. Was Pinkie's remark related to that newsreel?"

"In a way," Nick said.

"Was it directed at Franny personally?"

"No, sir. It was a general remark."

"Then you were distraught?"

"I guess so."

"Guess, hell. I'm not in the habit of submitting phony reports, Nick. If you were distraught, I'll say so, and you'll be off the hook. Otherwise, you can take your chances with the CO."

"Yes, sir. I was distraught. Franny had gone through a traumatic experience, and it affected me more deeply than I'd thought."

Dr. D'Amato lit a cigarette and tossed the pack to Nick.

"I've noticed your war journals, Nick," he said. "Trying to figure out how it all got started?"

"Yes, sir. Without much success."

"Well, I'll tell you, Nick." He crossed the room and sat down on an examining table. "Wars are no great mystery to me. I interned in Michigan when the casualties were pouring in from the sit-down strikes. It was a godawful war. Labor versus management. Men committed acts of cruelty and violence they'd normally deplore. And then on Saturday nights, the casualties would roll in from the domestic wars. Husbands and wives, fathers and sons, best friends. Terrible violence, some of it as bad as anything in Ward B. There are little wars all over the place, Nick. It's no surprise that now and again they erupt into a big war."

"And I just started a little war with Pinkie," Nick said. "It that what you're saying?"

"You figure it out." He took a small box from the pocket of his white coat, which, as usual, was spotted and smelled of ether. "Here, I was bringing this up to you when the call came in. It's a message pad. Keep it on your nightstand and write notes to Hildy, or something. As an excuse to practice your handwriting."

Nick smiled. "Hey, thanks, Doc," he said.

"One more thing," Dr. D'Amato said. "Don't lose any sleep over this." He winked. "Frankly, Pinkie can be a pain in the ass."

The episode of the newsreel had a lingering effect on Nick. Toward the end of July, the commanding officer announced that patients who had earned them would receive medals and citations from an assistant secretary of the Navy in a ceremony to be held the following Sunday, on the West Lawn. The announcement disturbed Nick. After Ward B and the newsreel, medals seemed a pretension. He was glad when Hildy declined to participate.

"It's a lot of crap, Nick," he said. "You know what they say about medals. With the Navy Cross and a nickel, you can ride the subway all day. Let's just stay up here and play checkers."

"Can we do that?" Nick asked Dr. D'Amato.

"Suit yourselves," he replied with a shrug. "You can have the brass pin them on you, or you can collect them via yard mail. I'll just tell the CO you're not up to it."

Franny was miffed.

"You're being silly, Nickie," she said. "At least let me get you a set of ribbons to wear on your uniform."

"Hildy says no fruit salad either," he said. "Try to understand, Franny. We're a team in this matter."

Franny sighed. "All right, all right," she said. "To paraphrase Voltaire, I disagree with what you're doing, but will oppose till death your right to do it."

"Oh, God," Nick said, and groaned. "I'm marrying a comedienne."

A few days after the ceremony, their medals and citations arrived in the yard mail, in large manila envelopes. Hildy tossed his into his seabag without opening it. Nick did likewise, but one night, when Hildy was asleep, he got out his envelope and examined the medals under the lamp on the card table.

They glittered in the lamplight and had a nice feel to them.

18. A SIGNATURE

HILDY'S SURGERY FAILED.

Dr. D'Amato, assisted by Miss Stritch, removed the cast on a hot August morning, in the Penthouse, using a rubber mallet and a stainless steel chisel and splitting the cast as neatly as a coconut. Under probing, Hildy's kneecap squirmed around like a bar of soap.

"I guess I ruined it when I took that fall," he said disappointment showing in his eyes.

"Not necessarily," Dr. D'Amato said. "Knees are tricky gadgets, Hildy. It's one thing when the ligaments are torn from the bone; it's another when the ligaments themselves are shredded as badly as yours. There was only an outside chance of success, even without the fall."

"What now, Doc?"

"Great Lakes. The sooner, the better. I'll get on the phone right away. Plan on leaving in ten days." He circled August 14 on the calendar. "You, too, Nick," he said over his shoulder. "Your stump is ready, and I'm sure

I can work you in at Bethesda by then. The two of you came here together; you may as well leave together."

"Yes, sir," Nick said.

"How do I get by in the meantime?" Hildy asked. "Another cast?"

"No. A brace. A temporary one for a few days. It'll be a little cumbersome, but you'll have a better device by the time you leave for Great Lakes."

"Will I need a crutch?"

"I doubt it. You'll have a stiff leg, but you should be able to manage fairly well with a cane. You might even be able to do some dancing Sunday."

"What's going on Sunday?" Nick asked.

"Haven't you heard about the big dance?" Dr. D'Amato said. "A USO orchestra, colored lights — the works. You'd better tell Franny."

Franny, it turned out, already knew about the dance.

"I called Diane," she told Nick. "Guess what. She's coming."

"I don't believe it," he said.

"I couldn't either. But don't get your hopes up. I think it's really over between them. She's got a gift for Hildy, a painting."

"Is she going to stay at your place?"

"No. She'll be visiting out on Long Island. Some artist friends she met in the Poconos."

"Well — " Nick said, raising an eyebrow. "It'll be interesting."

On August 6, President Truman announced that the United States had used a devastating new weapon — an atomic bomb — against Japan. A single bomb dropped on Hiroshima had obliterated the city and, presumably, killed most of its inhabitants.

"Atomic bomb?" Hildy said. "What's an atomic bomb?"

"I'm not sure," Nick said, and spent an hour in the library looking up such unfamiliar terms as "fission," "shock wave," "radioactivity." As he pored over the encyclopedia, images of the strike on the *Yamato* went through his mind — of Raspberry One roaring full-power over the Inland Sea, of the flak bursts that blackened the sky, and of Hiroshima in the distance — green, lovely, its black and red pagodas gleaming in the sun. And now it was gone. All of it.

"If a bomb like that doesn't end the war," Dr. D'Amato said when he and Miss Stritch stopped by the Penthouse later that day, "nothing will."

"I can't conceive of such slaughter," Miss Stritch said. "All of those people dead, and they probably had nothing to do with the war."

"I don't believe that for a minute, Miss Stritch," said Hildy, who was playing checkers with Franny. "They were in it up to their teeth. All of them."

"Hildy!" Miss Stritch said, surprised at the hardness of his attitude. "Surely you don't mean that."

Franny looked up from the checkerboard. "Do you think we should kiss and make up, Miss Stritch?" she said sharply. "I don't know who was in it or who wasn't. But after what happened in those Nazi camps, I don't think I could bear to hear a German accent ever again."

Miss Stritch turned to Nick, seeking moral support, but he lit a cigarette and turned away.

"War," she said with a sigh, and sat down on Hildy's bed. "I suppose you get inured to the horror of it."

She was right, Nick thought. A part of him wept for Hiroshima; another part, remembering boys with downy cheeks struggling against sharks, shed no tears. He hated the way he felt. War, he thought. It infected everything.

And yet three days later, when a second atomic bomb was dropped, this one on the city of Nagasaki in southern Japan, neither Nick nor Hildy paid much attention to the news. Nick was busy planning his schedule at Columbia; Hildy was phoning all over New York in a futile effort to get a reservation on the Twentieth Century Limited. He'd been issued a voucher for first-class rail accommodations to Great Lakes, but the famous streamliner, a favorite of movie stars and important businessmen, was booked six weeks in advance. Franny offered to help.

"Give me the voucher," she said. "One of my father's patients is a vice president of the New York Central."

"I doubt that even he could do any good," Hildy said. "The voucher's only good for a roomette, and the Century is mostly drawing rooms and compartments. There's only one car of roomettes."

"We'll see," Franny said. "I'll let you know at the dance."

The dance was held in the solarium, which was decorated with crepe paper streamers and flowers from the hospital gardens. Soft lights that changed from blue to pink to orchid played over the room, and there was a long refreshment table, covered in white, with fruit punch and cake and tiny open-faced sandwiches. The orchestra, a large one, had already begun the first set when Nick and Hildy came down from the Penthouse. Hildy spotted Dr. D'Amato dancing with Miss Stritch, both of them in dress uniform.

"Hey, Doc," he called to him, "that's quite a step you're doing. What's it called?"

"Ask Lieutenant Stritch," Dr. D'Amato called back. "She's leading" — and they laughed and danced off.

The orchestra filled the room with sweet music. The

floor was crowded with dancers. The girls — nurses, Red Cross volunteers, and neighborhood girls who attended hospital social functions out of a sense of patriotic duty. And the patients — some in uniform, others in robes and hospital gowns, some on crutches or canes, a few in wheelchairs, twirling about with great enjoyment. To an outsider, Nick thought, it might seem a grim gathering, but for the patients and medical staff, it was a gay occasion.

"There's Franny," Hildy said, pointing across the room.

Franny, wearing her gray uniform and carrying a tray of sandwiches, was moving through a section reserved for the commanding officer and his staff and for the men of Ward B, their wheelchairs and stretchers arranged to allow a full view of both the orchestra and the dance floor. Franny waved when she saw them.

"I'll be right over," she called. "Diane's not here yet."

But Diane was there, just arriving. Nick saw her come in from the lobby just as the orchestra began a medley of waltzes. Not quite the Diane they had left behind — a little thinner, her hair shorter, her features more serious, but still exciting and breathtakingly pretty, in a summery dress of pastel stripes, with white shoes and a corsage of white carnations. For the briefest moment, there was a frightened look in her eyes as she saw the crutches and canes, the amputees and burn cases. Then, with a smile, she crossed the floor to where Nick and Hildy were standing — and it was Quonset Point again.

"I don't have a dance card," she said to Hildy. "But I believe this is our waltz. Take his cane, Nick. He can lean on me."

And slowly, shyly, they glided out on the dance floor, Hildy not so much dancing as letting Diane dance around him. Franny had seen Diane come in and now was standing beside Nick.

"They're still a matched pair, aren't they?" she said, her eyes glistening.

"Yes," Nick said, smiling with pleasure. "Even scarred and half-crippled, he's still the all-American boy."

"Well," she said, tugging at the pinned-up sleeve that covered his stump, "what are we waiting for?"

Nick pointed to the orchestra. "Five saxophones," he said. "Not bad, eh?"

"Just like the casino," Franny said with a smile, and went into his arms.

During intermission, the four of them went through the refreshment line, then took their plates out to the veranda, where they talked eagerly of the future. Franny had been to a tea at Barnard and, while there, had scouted apartments in the Morningside Heights district.

"Rents are outrageous," she said. "They want a fortune for just one room and a kitchenette, and everyone says it'll get worse when the war ends. By the time we're married, we may not be able to afford a furnished room."

"You'll be poor," Diane said. "But that's all right; I'll still visit you."

"Bring wine and cheese," Nick said.

"And lox," Franny added.

Diane told them of her summer in the Poconos.

"I did nothing but paint," she said. "It's become my one and only interest."

She had been accepted to study for six weeks under a prominent artist at his studio out on Long Island. After that, she would enroll at an art school in Greenwich Village. There was no point in returning to Wickford; Franny wouldn't be there.

"I'd really like to study abroad," she said, "but with

Europe in rubble, that's out of the question. Anyway, no one knows how many of the really good painters survived the war."

"When are we going to see a sample of your work?" Hildy asked her.

"Tonight." She blushed. "I left a present for you out in the lobby. But don't you dare look at it till I've gone. You might not like it, and I'd be mortified."

When the orchestra resumed, Nick and Franny went back in and danced. Diane and Hildy strolled out onto the West Lawn, talking. They were gone for a long time.

"What could they be doing out there?" Nick asked Franny.

"Saying good-by to each other," she answered.

Nick thought about that for a moment, then nodded. "Yes," he said, "I think you're right."

The dance was nearly over when they finally returned to the solarium. The crowd was happy but tired. A few of the Ward B patients had fallen asleep. The orchestra was playing "Jersey Bounce," a popular swing number with a smooth rhythm.

"There's still time for a couple of dances," Nick said to Hildy. "For a guy with a game leg, you do pretty well."

"Naw, Nick," he said self-consciously, "the beat's too fast, and my jitterbugging days are over."

"Oh, no, they're not," Diane said, grabbing his cane and tossing it to Nick. "Come on, Hildy. Let's strut our stuff."

And to Nick and Franny's amazement, they started jitterbugging, doing a restrained version of the strenuous dance, but never missing a step. The other dancers formed a circle around them, clapping and cheering as Diane rocked her hips and laughed gaily. Then as Hildy twirled her into his arms, the beat slowed, and the orchestra went into "Moonlight Serenade," the dreamy Glenn Miller ballad that they all loved. And it seemed to Nick that the music was a signature to an important part of their lives. Once upon a time, they had danced in the snow and done crazy things. Now, with the war drawing to a close, there would be a new beginning.

"Oh, Nickie," Franny whispered in his ear, "thank God you're alive."

When the music stopped, they milled around the dance floor for a few minutes, enjoying the afterglow of a pleasant evening. Then a duty corpsman came in from the lobby and told Diane that her friends were waiting in the courtyard.

"Well — " she said, her eyes wet with tears.

She kissed each of them, promising to keep in touch. Then, purposely, she clasped Nick's pinned-up sleeve with one hand and, with the other, pressed a finger to Hildy's scar, at the point where it disfigured his smile.

"God bless you both," she said — and walked out of their lives.

They watched in silence as she crossed the floor and left the solarium. Nick waited for Hildy to say something that would ease the deep emotion they all felt — and he did.

"When I tell them about her back in Minnesota," he said, "do you think they'll believe me?"

"You seem very calm and collected," Nick said. "What were the two of you talking about all that time?"

"Forks in the road," Hildy replied. "You know something, Nick? Until tonight, I never realized how much I admire her."

Franny took Nick's hand.

"Come on, you're both tired," she said. "Why don't you go on up to the Penthouse. I'll get Diane's painting and bring it up later."

"Okay," Nick said, and smiled at her. "It was a nice dance, wasn't it?"

"Nice isn't the word," she replied. "Beautiful. It was a beautiful dance."

Diane's painting, which was done in oils on a wide canvas, left them speechless. It was of Raspberry One, its blue paint faded, its fuselage smudged by the smoke of battle, climbing through a layer of broken clouds. Far below, receding in the distance, was the suggestion of an aircraft carrier. There was a weariness to the airplane, a sadness, as though it were saying, "I've done my job. Now let me rest in the clouds." It was a simple scene, but it possessed a mystical power that deeply moved Nick, for it perfectly expressed how he and Hildy felt about their plane, about Mr. Scott, about the war. Hildy spread the canvas out on the card table, under the lamp.

"Remember that painting at the Biltmore?" he said. "The one above the bar?"

"Yes," Franny said. "She used to stare at it and vow that one day she'd paint like that."

"I wish she'd done two," Nick said.

"You can have a copy made, Nick," Hildy said. "I'll leave it with Franny. I can't be lugging a painting to Great Lakes. Besides, it belongs in New York."

Hildy stayed up the rest of the night, at the card table, in the dark, smoking cigarettes and staring out the window. Twice, Nick was wakened when he turned on the lamp to look at Diane's painting. Finally, at dawn, he heard Hildy's brace clanking as he limped to bed.

Nick hoped he wouldn't have bad dreams.

19. A BACKWARD LOOK

AUGUST 14, 1945, FELL ON A TUESDAY. IT WAS
a day that most Americans would remember for the rest
of their lives, as they remembered December 7, 1941, and
June 6, 1944. On August 14, the war ended.

Nick rose early that day. He was nervous about
Hildy's departure and wanted a few private moments to
collect his thoughts. He considered today the end of his
Naval career. Bethesda would be anticlimactic; when
Hildy's train left, it would be over, a closed book.

The gray light of dawn filtered into the Penthouse.
Hildy, who had had a restless night, was finally asleep.
His bad leg, which Dr. D'Amato had fitted with a new
brace for the trip to Great Lakes, protruded awkwardly
from under the covers. Nick, in his childish, left-handed
scrawl, left a note on the pad on the nightstand — "I'm
outside" — then tiptoed out into the corridor and went
down the fire staircase to the main floor. The aroma of
bacon frying came from the officers' mess. He cadged a
mug of coffee from one of the steward's mates and, still
in his pajamas and the USN robe he'd grown so fond of,
took it out to the West Lawn.

It was a balmy summer morning. The first rays of
the sun made an orange glow over the Narrows. He could
just make out that over on the Jersey shore, the GAS IS
BEST advertisement was gone, replaced by CALL FOR
PHILIP MORRIS! It was a good omen, Nick thought; he
would have to tell Franny about it. He wished she were
going to be here today, but she'd promised Mrs. Sweeney
to fill in at the settlement house, and her word was her

bond. Besides, she had Hildy's train ticket and reservation, and would be at Grand Central to see him off.

He strolled down the graveled path, through the rose garden, and around the beds of day lilies, taking his time, pausing to sip his coffee and to smell the roses. He was keenly aware of final things. The hospital had helped give focus to his future and perspective to his past. He would remember it gratefully.

"Saying good-by to the old place?" a voice called to him.

Nick turned around. It was Dr. D'Amato, coming down from the veranda, also with a mug of coffee.

"Sort of," he replied, smiling. "How'd you guess?"

"I was doing the same thing," Dr. D'Amato said. "My orders arrived yesterday. I'll be leaving Thursday."

"For discharge?"

"Not exactly. I've volunteered for a year of duty with the Veterans Administration, at a hospital in Chicago."

"A VA hospital?" Nick said. "I'd have thought you'd be eager to get back to private practice."

"Oh, I am." He offered Nick a cigarette and lit one himself. "But — it's hard to explain, Nick. I suppose it's a matter of living with myself. If I hadn't been in medicine, I could easily have ended up in Ward B."

Nick was surprised that his thinking so closely paralleled his own. "I know what you mean," he said, feeling a new respect for him. "That's how I feel about the strike on the *Yamato*. You wonder why you were spared."

They strolled down to the seawall. Thin layers of mist hung over Ellis Island and the Statue of Liberty.

"I feel my roots stirring whenever I come down here," Dr. D'Amato said. "My mother and father came through Ellis Island around the turn of the century."

"So did Franny's," Nick said.

"From Europe?"

"The Ukraine."

"That must have taken real courage," Dr. D'Amato said. "My father had three dollars and the clothes on his back, and here I am forty years later, a physician."

He folded his arms and leaned back against the wrought-iron railing.

"Do you know what the word 'wop' means, Nick?" he asked.

"I didn't know it meant anything," Nick said, "except as a slur against Italians."

"But it really isn't," Dr. D'Amato said. "You see, during the great wave of immigration, few of them had passports. And so when they arrived at Ellis Island, their papers were stamped WOP, in caps."

"Without Passport?" Nick said.

"Correct. My father taught us that it was something to be proud of. He was a tailor. He worked his fingers raw, putting me through medical school. And when I think of all the immigrant fathers who slaved to put their sons through college, only to have them killed in the war — well, I feel an obligation."

"And so you're going to Chicago," Nick said.

"Yes. I'm going to Chicago to see if I can make things a bit easier for the basket cases."

"You won't be far from Great Lakes."

"Don't worry. I'll look in on Hildy and make sure they're doing right by him."

"Hey, that's great," Nick said. "He'll be glad to see a friendly face."

Dr. D'Amato glanced at his watch. "This has been very pleasant, Nicholas," he said. "But duty calls, as they say in the movies."

"Sir — " Nick said. "Our first night here, you said it was a privilege to have us as your patients. Well, I want you to know that it's been a privilege having you as our doctor."

"Thank you, Nick." Dr. D'Amato smiled and clasped Nick's left hand. "Let's stay in touch. I'll want to know of your progress."

Nick and Hildy had anticipated a leisurely day. Hildy's train wouldn't leave till six; Nick could catch any of the night trains to Washington. But checking out of a Naval hospital, they discovered, was not a simple matter. Each was required to undergo a complete physical — blood tests, neurological tests, even barium tests for gastric disorders.

"Regulations," Dr. D'Amato told them. "We don't like to export unknown problems to other hospitals."

There were delays in X ray and in Cardiology, and the lab work wasn't completed until two o'clock, after which there was another problem. The pants of Hildy's dress whites wouldn't fit over the new brace.

"I'll slit the seam," he said to Dr. D'Amato. "The way I did before."

"Not on your life," Dr. D'Amato replied. "You're not going to ride the Twentieth Century Limited in a tattered uniform" — and he sent the trousers down to the tailor shop to be let out, which left Hildy stranded in the Penthouse in his skivvies, inasmuch as their heavy luggage had been sent on ahead, Hildy's to Grand Central, Nick's to Penn Station.

"I feel like I'm getting ready for a high school dance," Hildy said, and grinned. "And my mom's down in the kitchen pressing my pants."

All that day, Nick had been noticing little flashes of

the old Hildy, an occasional grin, a slight sparkle in his eyes, a more cheerful outlook.

"They'd better hurry with your pants," he said. "I told Franny we'd be at Grand Central by five-thirty."

"It was swell of her dad to get me that reservation."

"Yes, it was. Too bad Diane won't be there to see you off. You know, the last stand of the old foursome."

"No, Nick," Hildy said, shaking his head. "It's better this way. I'll never forget those good times at Quonset Point, but we just weren't cut out for each other."

"You sure made a fine couple."

"Maybe we did," Hildy said. "At the casino or dancing in a club car. But you know something, Nick? I knew before the *Shiloh* even cleared the Panama Canal that Diane and I weren't any good for the long haul. It's as if certain people are good for each other at certain times, and when those times are over, it just doesn't work."

"No regrets, then?" Nick asked him.

"Regrets?" Hildy smiled fondly. "Heck no. Diane's as swell a girl as I'll ever meet. She's going to be an important artist one day, and maybe I'll have had something to do with it."

"Hildy," Nick said, throwing an arm around him, "what am I going to do without you?"

"The same thing I am, I guess. Tough it out."

Finally, at four o'clock, they were ready to leave — shoes shined, hats squared, overnight bags packed. Nick managed to knot his neckerchief with his left hand. "Not bad for a fledgling southpaw, eh?" he said, winking. Already, the Penthouse seemed empty, the beds stripped, the nightstand cleared, the checkerboard gone. Hildy took a long look around the room.

"I've grown attached to this glorified mop closet," he said.

"Did you get a souvenir?"

"Yeah. A checker."

"Red or black?"

"Black."

"I took a red one," Nick said, and they both laughed.

There was a clatter out in the corridor, and then Miss Stritch came through the doorway, followed by Dr. D'Amato, who was pushing a medicine cart laden with mugs of coffee, thick slices of angel food cake — and gifts.

"Holy cow, Doc!" Hildy exclaimed. "A party!"

"It's the least we could do," Dr. D'Amato said, and embraced the two of them in a big hug. "You boys have given us an excuse to get away from it all now and then, to have a smoke, a few laughs — "

"And play checkers," Miss Stritch put in.

"Yes, and play checkers," he said with a laugh. "Now, there isn't much time. Miss Stritch, if you'll please go first."

Miss Stritch took a little box from the cart and opened it.

"We want you to wear these with pride," she said, pinning sets of military ribbons to each of their uniforms.

For Hildy, there was the Purple Heart, the Distinguished Flying Cross, the Pacific campaign ribbon with two stars, the Air Medal, the Presidential Citation, and the Navy Cross; for Nick, an identical set, minus the Navy Cross.

Nick thought surely Hildy would politely unpin the ribbons; instead, he moved to the little wall mirror and saluted himself.

"Boy!" he said, letting out a whistle. "They're really impressive, all lined up together. How did we manage to accumulate this mess of fruit salad, Nick?"

"It was our fear of sharks," Nick replied, relieved that Hildy had accepted the ribbons, and everybody laughed.

Dr. D'Amato's gift to Nick was in a large carton.

"It's government property," he said to him. "Take a peek, and then pretend you never saw it."

Nick raised the lid; it was his *USN* hospital robe.

"Hey, Doc, I really appreciate this," he said, breaking into a wide smile. "It's the best robe I've ever had."

"You should see the rag he wears at home," Hildy said.

"I'll have it laundered and mailed to Philadelphia," Dr. D'Amato said, and then handed a narrow carrying case to Hildy. "This is a collapsible crutch, Hildy. You might get into a situation where the cane isn't adequate."

He spread the aluminum components out on the floor to show Hildy how to assemble them, and as he did so, a Red Cross volunteer ran into the room.

"The war's over! The President was just on the radio!" she yelled — and ran out again.

They looked at each other in disbelief. The news had been expected almost hourly since the bombing of Hiroshima, but now that it had come, they couldn't quite absorb it. Loud cheers were going up from every corner of the hospital. Outside, fireworks were exploding over the New Jersey skyline. Church bells were ringing from every direction, and the harbor was erupting in a blare of whistles and horns.

"It's really over," Dr. D'Amato said in a whisper. "Thank God."

And then he was on his feet, giving orders to Miss Stritch.

"Call the Shore Patrol and tell them to send over a wagon immediately. Traffic will be a mess, and these boys have less than an hour to get to Grand Central."

"I saw an SP wagon out in the courtyard," she said. "I'll make them wait."

"Good. And on your way back, stop at the pharmacy. In the refrigerator, at the back of the bottom shelf, there's a bottle of champagne wrapped in a towel. I've been saving it for this occasion."

It was a bottle of Mumm's, '37 — "a very good year," Dr. D'Amato said. Hildy poured the coffee down the utility sink and rinsed the mugs. Miss Stritch poured the champagne, and Dr. D'Amato gave a toast.

"To the white crosses everywhere," he said as they raised their mugs. "And to our country. Let freedom ring."

Nick felt tears come into his eyes. Nearly six years since Hitler invaded Poland; forty-four months since Pearl Harbor. The devastation was stupefying. Half the world lay in ruins. Whole populations were homeless. The war journals estimated the dead at forty million, perhaps fifty. He thought of the waste. Scholars, farmers, athletes, engineers, surgeons — all lost. The great books that would never be written, the great inventions that would never be thought up, the great statesmen who would never rise to leadership. And for what? He didn't know. One day he would; he was sure of it. But for now, all he knew was that the country was safe — and all its little pieces.

"It's all right, Nick," Miss Stritch said, and put an arm around him. "You can cry if you want."

And he did. They all did. And laughing and crying,

they moved as an entourage down the corridor to the elevator, and then across the lobby to the main entrance, where a Shore Patrol command car, its red lights flashing, was waiting. Nick noticed Pinkie hanging around the SP car and tried to avoid him, but Pinkie hurried up to him and shyly handed him a little package.

"It's a going-away present," he said.

Nick held the package against his chest with his stump and opened it with his left hand. It was a heavy glass paperweight, a globe, with an Alpine scene inside the glass — pine trees, snowdrifts, a rustic mountain cabin.

"The snow swirls when you jiggle it," Pinkie said. "You can use it to hold down the pages when you're reading."

"Thanks, Pinkie." Nick smiled and shook his hand warmly. "I'll always keep it."

"It's been swell knowing you, Nick," Pinkie said, opening the car door for him. "Take good care of yourself."

And then, with lights flashing and siren wailing, the SP car screeched away from the hospital.

"Good-by!" Dr. D'Amato and Miss Stritch called. "Good luck!"

As the car turned into the street, Nick had his last glimpse of the hospital — the courtyard, the porticoes, the marigolds blooming around the flagpole. Another image etched indelibly in his mind, he thought, as the war faded into his personal history.

"You know something, Nick?" Hildy said. "Taking a backward look, we've waved good-by to an awful lot of good people over the past two years."

New York was going wild with celebration. Confetti floated down from the skyscrapers, and flags unfurled everywhere. People were dancing in the streets and jamming the intersections. Times Square was a mass of reveling civilians and servicemen.

"Don't worry, boys," the driver, a burly CPO, said grimly. "We'll make it."

And they did, with seven minutes to spare. Franny was waiting in the main concourse of the great railroad terminal, at the information booth, frantic with worry.

"Oh, thank God," she said with a sigh of relief. "I was afraid you'd gotten stuck in traffic. The town's a madhouse."

She took Hildy's bags, which Nick was carrying, and waved to a redcap. "Please take these to the Twentieth Century Limited," she told him. "Drawing room B, car three twenty-four."

Hildy looked at her in confusion. "A drawing room?" he said.

"It's my father's treat," Franny said, steering them toward the train gate. "He said that, with your leg, you'll need more space than just a roomette."

"Gee, Franny, that's swell of him. Tell him how much I appreciate it."

"He already knows that, Hildy." She handed him his ticket and for the first time noticed his ribbons. "I don't believe it!" she cried. "You're wearing fruit salad!"

"Yeah," Hildy said anxiously. "What do you think?"

"Very debonair," she said. "No, not debonair. Very heroic."

"Franny," Nick said, "there are no heroes in a war. Just guys who are afraid of — "

"Nickie," she said, "if you feed me that line about the sharks one more time, I'll brain you."

"What's wrong with the shark line?" Hildy said. "I

plan on using it when I get to the university. You know, limping around the campus with my scar and my medals." He went into a little act. " 'No, m'dear, I wasn't a hero, just afraid of sharks.' The girls will fall all over me."

Franny was in stitches, and Nick could tell that she, too, was noticing glimmers of the old Hildy. "You're really glad to be going back, aren't you, Hildy?" she said.

"Yes, Franny, I really am. I guess I had to come east to find out I belong in Minnesota."

"I nearly forgot," she said. "I still have your kitty of unused train tickets. What should I do with them?"

"Cash them in and give the money to Mrs. Sweeney," Hildy suggested. "Is that okay with you, Nick?"

"Yes, that's fine," Nick said, and laughed. "Remember the victory party we talked about having at the Biltmore? We were going to drink a toast and smash the glasses in the fireplace."

"Did we really talk about doing that?" Hildy shook his head ruefully. "Smashing glasses in a fireplace. It seems kind of silly now, doesn't it?"

"A lot of things seem silly now," Nick said.

At the train gate, the attendant urged Hildy to hurry aboard.

"She's about ready to roll, son," he said.

"Yes, sir," Hildy said. "I'll just be a second."

And then slowly, reluctantly, he turned to face Nick and Franny.

"Well, Nick," he said, "we've come a long way."

Nick was so choked up, he could hardly talk. "You kept me alive, Hildy," he said, hugging his friend.

"We kept each other alive, Nick. Knowing you has been the greatest experience of my life."

He reached an arm out to Franny.

"Franny," he said. "They don't come any better than you."

Franny stood on her toes and kissed him.

"It's been so very good knowing you, Hildy," she said, making no effort to hide her tears. "Do us proud out in Minnesota."

"I'll try, Franny. I'll really try."

He turned and started through the gate. And as Nick watched him limping down the ramp to the train, he understood what Hildy had tried to tell him in the Penthouse. Theirs had been a wartime friendship; now each would have to find his way alone.

The gate slammed shut. Franny took his hand.

"Come on," she said. "I'm taking you home. We'll sip wine and look out over the city."

"I can't believe he's gone," Nick said.

"Do you think we'll ever see him again?"

"Well, we've got Raspberry One. Sooner or later, he's going to want to see it."

"I've got an idea," Franny said.

"What?"

"The Twentieth Century Limited has a radio-telephone. He'll be in Syracuse around eleven. Let's call him up and tell him we love him."

"What a great idea!" Nick said. "He'll know we're not letting go. You're full of good ideas, do you know that?"

"Naturally," she said, and smiled. "I'm a Wickford girl."

They crossed the concourse and went out into the balmy New York evening.

The war was over.

GLOSSARY

Air Plot
A carrier's flight control center. It monitors the position of, and maintains communication with, all airborne aircraft.

Angels
The altitude of an aircraft in thousands of feet. "Angels five" means five thousand feet, and so on.

Arrested Landing System
A hydraulic system for arresting the speed of aircraft landing aboard a carrier. A plane's tail hook engages one of several steel "arresting wires" (cables) stretched across the flight deck. Like a rubber band, it becomes taut, which brings the plane to a gradual stop.

Bandit
An enemy fighter plane. Not to be confused with "bogey," which is an unidentified plane.

Barrier
Steel cables raised across the flight deck during aircraft recovery, like a tennis net, to halt aircraft that fail to engage an arresting wire.

Blinker
A means for transmitting Morse code by a light that flashes on and off. Long flashes mean dashes; short ones, dots.

Blip
An image on a radar scope.

Bogey
An unidentified aircraft.

CINCPAC
Commander in Chief, Pacific Fleet. (In 1945, this was Admiral Chester W. Nimitz.)

Combat Air Patrol (CAP)
Fighter aircraft that patrol the sky above a carrier to protect the ship from attack.

Combat Information Center (CIC)
Nerve center of a warship's combat operations, directing all elements of the ship's combat potential.

CPO
Chief petty officer.

Decommission
To remove from service a naval vessel or unit.

General Quarters (GQ)
Battle stations.

Intercom
An aircraft's intercommunication system.

Kamikaze
Literally, "divine wind." In World War II, it meant a Japanese aircraft, heavily loaded with explosives, that was flown in "suicide" crashes onto ships and other targets.

Landing Signals Officer (LSO)
The officer who, by the use of luminous signal paddles, directs an approaching aircraft to a landing on a carrier. He is stationed on a small platform, to port, at the aft end of the flight deck.

Mae West
An inflatable life jacket worn by American airmen in World War II.

Ready Room
In an aircraft carrier, the headquarters of a combat squadron. The room in which pilots and crews are briefed, await orders, store their flight gear, relax.

Scope (Radar)
A cathode ray tube, or a screen, calibrated for distance and direction, on which radar images appear.

Scuttlebutt
Rumor or gossip.

Ship's Company
The regular crew of a ship. Air groups were assigned to a carrier on a temporary, irregular basis, and thus were not considered to be ship's company.

Splash!
The term used to indicate an enemy plane shot down over water.

Strike
Attack by air. Can be used as a noun ("They are planning a strike") or as a verb ("They will strike").

Vector

A course or direction. Can be used as a noun ("My vector is north") or as a verb ("I will vector north").

VHF

Very high frequency. This was the radio band used by carrier planes for voice transmission. Its range was limited.

V-mail

In World War II, lightweight, single-sheet, stationery used in overseas correspondence to and from servicemen. The letters were reduced photographically before being transmitted.